Physical
Evidence

Books by Thomas T. Noguchi, M.D., and Arthur Lyons

Unnatural Causes

Books by Thomas T. Noguchi, M.D.

Coroner

Coroner at Large

Jacob Asch books by Arthur Lyons

All God's Children

The Dead are Discreet

The Killing Floor

Dead Ringer

Castles Burning

Hard Trade

At the Hands of Another

Three With a Bullet

Fast Fade

Other People's Money

Physical Evidence

Thomas T. Noguchi, M.D.
and
Arthur Lyons

G. P. Putnam's Sons
New York

G. P. Putnam's Sons
Publishers Since 1838
200 Madison Avenue
New York, NY 10016

Published simultaneously in Canada

This is a work of fiction. The events described are imaginary, and the characters are fictitious and not intended to represent actual persons.

Library of Congress Cataloging-in-Publication Data

Noguchi, Thomas T., date.
Physical evidence / Thomas T. Noguchi and Arthur Lyons.
p. cm.
I. Lyons, Arthur. II. Title.
PS3564.0354P47 1990 89-28636 CIP
813'.54–dc20
ISBN 0-399-13530-8

Printed in the United States of America

1 2 3 4 5 6 7 8 9 10

This book has been printed on acid-free paper.

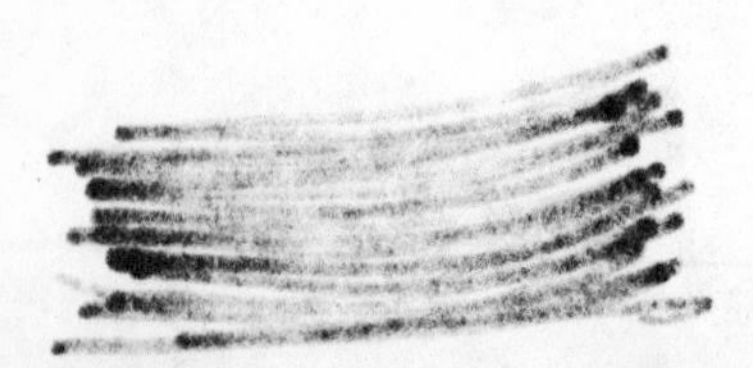

Acknowledgments

We would like to give special thanks to Tom Ardies, Dr. Chuck Garrison, Bill Lystrup, William McMullin, Don Wykoff, Dr. Stephen Kopp, and Dr. Lawrence Cone for their aid in researching this book.

To Cathy and Boomer
who brought love and joy to my life,
and for my best friend
the highly respected Forensic Odontologist,
Professor Kazuo Suzuki
of the Tokyo Dental College,
and fellow members of the Medicolegal Society of Japan

—TN

Prologue

ONCE, YEARS AGO, SHE had been a great beauty, with long, thick hair as black as pitch, and large, dark eyes that smoldered with a fierce pride and courage. But the last few years of her disease had been cruel, and now the hair was wispy and gray, the once-firm flesh hung loosely on the high cheekbones, the eyes were sunken and shriveled in their sockets. But the disease had not been satisfied merely sucking away her beauty and strength; it wanted more. It wanted everything: her pride, her dignity, her life.

The pentobarbital had quieted the spasms that had wracked the woman's frail body, and her expression looked peaceful, relaxed. Gabriel watched the woman's chest rise and fall rhythmically as the respirator pumped oxygen into her lungs.

All in all, pre-op prep had gone smoothly. The endotracheal tube had been placed in the patient's throat and hooked up to the portable heart-lung unit without event. They had a bit of a problem locating the femoral artery in the right leg, but once they had, the artery and vein had been raised and cannulated without any major problem, and the lines connected to the portable blood pump and bubble oxygenator, which for the next few hours would function as the woman's heart, pumping oxygen-rich blood through her body. After being packed in ice to bring down her body temperature, the patient had been transported for surgery, where she now awaited the arrival of the doctor.

Gabriel turned to one of the other two surgical assistants in the room and snapped: "You said Dr. Katsilometes is scrubbed?"

"Yes, sir," the man replied nervously. He was quite short and seemed menaced by Gabriel's tall, thin frame, which towered over him. "He said he'd be right in."

Gabriel muttered something inaudible through his mask, shook his head angrily. Katsilometes had been called over an hour ago, and every minute the procedure was delayed reduced the patient's chances. There was no goddamn excuse for this, although Gabriel knew that Katsilometes would have one, as usual. The man was a screw-up, but there was nothing that could be done about that now. Few other doctors had performed this kind of surgical procedure before, and few others would even be willing to try.

At that moment, the doors of the operating room opened and Katsilometes strode in briskly. Through his surgical mask, he said reproachfully to Gabriel: "I hope you realize, Jeremy, that you broke up the best winning streak I've had in five years of Monday night poker."

Gabriel held his temper. "Sorry for the inconvenience."

"Everything ready to go?" Katsilometes asked cheerfully, seemingly oblivious to the chill in the other man's voice.

"It's been ready for half an hour."

The rebuke was unmistakable, but the doctor seemed unaffected. "There is one primary rule in life that takes precedence over all others, Jeremy. Never leave a straight flush. What's the patient's core temperature?"

The second surgical assistant moved to the foot of the table and checked the rectal probe. "Twelve-point-eight Centigrade."

"Oxygenation?"

"One hundred percent," Gabriel said.

The doctor nodded and selected a scalpel from the stainless-steel tray beside the operating table. "Well, Mrs. Wechsler, we knew it would come to this eventually."

This was only the second open-heart surgery Katsilometes had performed, but he worked quickly, confidently, and within twenty minutes had opened the patient's chest and had the retractor in place, exposing the woman's heart, which was now still, its work load being performed by the blood pump. He was cross-clamping the aortic root when he glanced at the woman's face and was shocked to notice that she seemed to be grimacing around the seal of the endotracheal tube. His eyes were wide, whites showing all the way around the irises, as he looked sharply at Gabriel. "This woman is alive!"

"Don't be silly," Gabriel said.

"Look at her face, goddamn it!" the doctor said, his voice close to panic. "She's in pain!"

Gabriel, unruffled, moved to the head of the table and took a closer look. The woman's eyes were pinched together, the muscles around her mouth were clamped tight on the tracheal tube. He fixed the alarmed surgeon with a steadying stare. "It's just an involuntary muscular contraction. The woman is dead, Doctor. I guarantee it."

Gabriel filled a syringe with 1.5 grams of sodium pentobarbital and injected the anesthetic into the three-way valve on the I.V. line that ran into June Wechsler's arm. The woman's grimacing ceased almost immediately. "Proceed, Doctor."

Katsilometes' eyes still looked uncertain, but he nodded. His hands trembled slightly as he continued the procedure. By the time he had finished clamping the aorta and tying off the veins and arteries that ran from the heart, his forehead was damp with perspiration.

The pump, which substituted as the woman's heart, was shut off, and Katsilometes cut the carotid and vertebral arteries above the silk ties, letting the blood from the severed vessels drain into the line that ran into a bucket beneath the table. He was bent over the table, hooking up the catheter to the perfusion unit, when the woman's heart sprang suddenly to life. The pressure of the arrhythmic beating caused the silk tie on the right vertebral artery to blow and blood spurted out of the artery as if from a high-pressure garden hose, into Katsilometes' face.

"Jesus Christ!" the surgeon exclaimed, reeling backward, temporarily blinded. Another stream of blood shot by him, hitting the tiled wall of the operating room, four feet away.

"Clamp, goddamn it!"

A clamp was slapped in his hand and he managed to pinch off the open artery without further loss of blood, after which he turned, shaken and blood-spattered, to Gabriel. "I told you this woman was alive!"

Gabriel said quietly: "And I'm telling you she's brain-dead. Her EEG was completely flat."

"Look—"

"*You* look," Gabriel said, taking two steps over to the respirator. He turned off the machine and the woman's chest stopped moving. "She is not breathing on her own. Her brain is history."

Katsilometes shook his head and said in a tremulous voice: "I won't be a party to this—"

"You already *are* a party to this," Gabriel said frostily. "Just complete the procedure. Unless you think you can put everything back together and revive her." He hit the switch and the lungs began to inflate smoothly once more.

The two men stared at each other for a long moment.

"We're wasting precious time, Doctor," Gabriel said quietly. "Every moment we waste, cells are dying."

Katsilometes sighed in resignation, then moved slowly back to the table. With bloody, shaking hands, he attached the lines running from the hemodialysis pump to the vertebral and carotid arteries and at 0657 hours, the solution of mannitol, glucose, and salts began to be pumped from the large plastic container beside the table, into the patient's brain.

For two hours, the machine hummed steadily, replacing the woman's blood with the salt-glucose mixture, while the technicians went about their work, monitoring gauges and running periodic checks on pH and calcium levels. At 0859 hours, perfusion was complete and the pump was shut off. It was time for the final phase of the operation. Katsilometes took a deep breath. "Ready for cephalic isolation."

With a #11 scalpel, Katsilometes began the incision, slicing deeply through muscle and connective tissue on both sides of the patient's neck, joining the cuts posteriorly just below the junction of the fifth and sixth cervical vertebrae. The incision complete, he exchanged the scalpel for a stryker electric saw. The whine of the saw turned to a high-pitched grinding as the blade cut through the spinal cord, and the room was instantly filled with the hot, acrid odor of burning bone.

Katsilometes put down the saw. Carefully, he picked up the woman's head and deposited it into the double polyethylene bag held open by Gabriel. Gabriel lifted the bag and peered through the plastic at the head. "Perfect," he said, his voice registering satisfaction. The blue eyes turned to the exhausted, blood-stained figure of Katsilometes. "Nice job, Doctor."

Twenty minutes later, Gabriel pushed open the doors of the operating room and was immediately set upon by the woman's son, who had been pacing the hallway floor like a caged animal for the past three hours. The man's eyes were watery and red from lack of sleep. "How is she?" he asked anxiously.

Gabriel pulled off his surgical mask. His face was long and pale. Strands of white hair poked out from underneath his green cap. He put a hand on the distraught son's shoulder and smiled reassuringly: "She's fine. The operation was a complete success."

"Can I see her?"

Gabriel raised an eyebrow questioningly. "Are you sure you want to?"

"Yes."

Gabriel shrugged his assent and beckoned the son to follow.

A curtain had been pulled across the operating table.

Sounds could be heard behind the curtain as the two assistants sutured and stapled, preparing the body for transport. Gabriel paid no attention to the sounds as he led the other man to a nearby table. On the table, a three-foot-high cylindrical container stood, its polished surface gleaming brightly in the harsh glare of the overhead fluorescent lights.

The son stared at the container for a moment in stunned silence, then reached out and touched the container hesitantly. Its metal surface was cold, unyielding. He looked up at the tall man with tear-filled eyes. "Do you think it would be possible to be alone with her? Just for a minute?"

Gabriel said nothing, but nodded understandingly. He went behind the curtain and the doctor and the two gowned assistants followed him outside.

The room was silent now, except for the faint electrical buzz of the fluorescents. The son placed both hands on the cylinder and bent down. He closed his eyes and gently put his cheek against the cold metal. "I love you, mom," he murmured, over and over again.

One

JIM "NOBODY SKATES" GORDON was standing impatiently near Vickman's crowded counter, a rapacious hunger in his eyes, a dead cigar wedged into the corner of his mouth. A man of appetites, Parker mused. The cigar would not be removed until he had food to replace it.

Gordon was a short, stocky, forty-six-year-old Deputy D.A. Three, who, for the twelve years Parker had known him, had been waging an onrunning battle with the same fifteen pounds of excess weight, an addiction to Cuban cigars, and the internal political machinations of the Los Angeles D.A.'s office. He was a maverick, which was why, after putting in sixteen years successfully prosecuting felons, he had been repeatedly bypassed for promotion. It was also why he and Parker got along so well.

The attitude of most of Gordon's superiors was that he was "not a team player," an irascible and bothersome malcontent. In an atmosphere that placed the highest value on politically expedient behavior, he was tolerated only because he was a rarity in his profession—competent. Sharp attorneys who went to work for the D.A.'s office usually didn't stick around long, using the job as a stepping stone to the big bucks of private practice, and the ones that stayed often did so because of political ambitions, or because they were too incompetent to make it on the outside.

Gordon was an exception. He was a brilliant, ruthless prosecutor, who stayed because he liked what he did. He often talked about leaving the office (about as often as he talked about giving up cigars), but deep down, he knew it was just talk. To many attorneys, justice was just a game and it didn't matter on what side they played, as long as they won. But though he would never admit it for fear of being called an idealist, with Jim Gordon, justice was a passion. No matter how much more money he could be making by putting skates on the scum he prosecuted, he knew he could never do it and live with himself.

A caged lion, Parker thought, watching the man pace. He wondered what would happen if, very soon now, someone didn't throw him some meat. His need was almost tactile. It cried out. Parker himself was very much an opposite of the stocky prosecutor, tall and lean, his brown hair liberally salted with gray, his smooth, boyish face making him appear much younger than his forty-three years. There was, unwittingly, more deception about him. You couldn't know him all at once.

"This is hard to watch," Parker said, stepping up behind Gordon. "What happens if they don't feed you?"

"I eat *them,*" Gordon growled. He pumped Parker's hand and gestured him toward the counter, where a line of cooks served the fare of the day to the assortment of businessmen and women, city attorneys, politicians, and other city, state, and county employees, who jammed into Vickman's every noon hour for a quick, good, and inexpensive lunch.

"Sorry I'm late."

"Hey," Gordon said amiably. "I'm honored that a world-renowned forensic pathologist like yourself would take time out of his schedule to have lunch. I know how busy you must be."

Parker winced. Gordon had a propensity to needle people early in any encounter. He apparently thought putting them on the defensive gave him an advantage. That, quite possibly, was another personality trait that had held him back at the office.

"You've lost some weight," Parker remarked, a sure way of scoring points with Gordon.

Gordon patted his belly and tugged at his belt. "About eight pounds. Had to. Three months ago—right before Christmas—I went in for a checkup and found out my blood pressure was up ten points. My doc said, 'Twenty points, that's it.' So I've been speed-walking four miles a day and watching the fats."

"Looks like it's paying off," Parker said sincerely.

"Yeah, but this last twelve are the tough ones. I figure it'll take until Memorial Day to get 'em off. Then you'll see a new me. Jim Gordon—Hunter-Gatherer."

"How about the cigars?"

Gordon held up two fingers. "I limit myself to two a day. One in the car when I go to work in the morning, the other at night when I go home."

"Sounds like a good plan," Parker observed.

The D.A. nodded. "Aside from helping my health, I'm striking a blow for the security of the western hemisphere. Without my support, I figure Castro will fall within a year."

They got to the front of the line and the henna-haired woman behind the counter said pleasantly: "The swordfish is good today, Jim."

"You've convinced me," Gordon said. "With cottage cheese and iced tea."

Parker told her to make it two and the woman dropped the two luncheon plates onto their trays. "Twelve-sixty."

Parker started to pull out his wallet, but Gordon stopped him with a shake of his head. "I asked you to lunch." He gave the woman a twenty and tipped her two dollars from the change, and they took their trays to one of the few empty tables.

When they had gotten settled, Parker asked: "So how are things around the D.A.'s office?"

Gordon shrugged impassively. "About the same. You hear that Rheinhold is going to step down to run for State A.G.?"

Parker nodded and tried the swordfish. It was delicious. "Who's going to be the front-runner for D.A.?"

"Probably Garth Meyers. That dumb bitch Lauren Forello has been making noises about running."

"The one who handled the Anderson Preschool molestation case?"

"The same."

"She sure botched up that case."

"Yep. And if she gets in as D.A., she's going to botch up a hell of a lot more. The woman is a major idiot."

"Has she got a chance?"

He shrugged. "Dan Quayle is our vice president. Need I say more?" Gordon's expression turned serious and Parker guessed that signaled the end of the small talk. The guess was confirmed when the prosecutor said: "You're going to testify for the defense at the Ennis trial, I hear."

"That's right."

"You know about Ennis?"

"I know he's a convicted felon, if that's what you're getting at."

Gordon nodded and opened his attaché case. He took out a piece of paper and began to read. "Lamar Harold Ennis, male cauc, DOB 1-9-59. Drifter, part-time welder, part-time auto mechanic. First arrest at the age of eleven for vandalism and cruelty to animals. Used to like to light fire to the neighbors' dogs and watch them run around. Served twelve months in CYA at the age of thirteen, after he assaulted his mother with a hatchet. His parents were divorced and Harry was released to the custody of his father, after his mother decided she didn't need any more scars. He spent three of the next five years back in CYA, for assorted violations—runaway, shoplifting, burglary.

"Arrested, aggravated assault, 11-23-79, charges dropped 'in the interest of justice.' Arrested 4-6-81, aggravated assault and rape. Charges dropped when victim changed her testimony. The detectives think the girl was intimidated by Ennis—"

"That is speculation on their part—"

Gordon held up his hand and went on. "Two years later, Ennis was picked up on the same charge. Same result. Six months later, he was arrested again, same charge. While Ennis was out on bail, the victim, Gloria Handel, disappeared. She was never found. Police suspected foul play, but without the girl's testimony, they had no choice but to cut Ennis loose. There wasn't enough physical evidence to make a case.

"Eighteen months ago, Ennis was arrested in Barstow for the kidnap and rape-murder of sixteen-year-old Jeanette Wilson, a high school student. Just like in the Beckworth case, the girl's Achilles tendons had been cut, so she couldn't get away. She was tortured with pliers, repeatedly raped and sodomized, then strangled. The body was found out in the desert, six days later, at least what was left of it. The scavengers had taken parts of it."

Parker started to comment, but Gordon held up his hand. "Ennis was arrested after a witness said he'd seen the girl get into a dark-colored van driven by a man matching Ennis's description. He was tried and acquitted. The case, like Beckworth, was based almost entirely on circumstantial evidence, most of it forensic, but the jury apparently didn't think it was compelling enough to send a man to death row. Part of the problem was that a lot of the physical evidence was destroyed by the elements. Part of it was a series of fuck-ups at the crime scene by the San Berdoo sheriffs."

Gordon reached into his attaché case, took out a fat manila envelope, and put it on the table in front of Parker.

Parker eyed it. "What's that?"

"The coroner's report on Wilson."

"What am I supposed to do with it?"

"Read it."

"What for? You said Ennis was acquitted."

"That doesn't mean he didn't do it."

"What's the difference? He can't be tried again for it."

"That's precisely why I want you to read it."

"It's not going to change my testimony," Parker said. "I'm a scientist. All I can do is offer an opinion, based on the evidence. How much weight the jury gives that opinion, or the evidence, is out of my hands."

"What *is* your opinion?"

Parker shrugged. "It's a game of percentages, you know that. The semen found in Sally Beckworth could have come from Ennis. It also could have come from fourteen percent of the male Caucasian population."

"And the hair and fibers that were found on the body?"

"The hair was a partial. It's almost worthless, you know that. The most anybody can say about it is it could have come from Ennis's head. The fibers were consistent with carpet fibers in the back of Ennis's van, but they were also consistent with fibers in all Dodge vans of that year. Ennis could have killed her. So could a lot of other men. What weight the jury gives all that, against the fact that Ennis's alibi—"

"His alibi is shit," Gordon sneered. "It all revolves around time of death."

"Which Dr. Fernell estimated at approximately seven P.M."

"He has since revised that estimate."

"That'll go over well in court."

Gordon smiled slyly. "What about the boot prints and the tire impressions at the scene?"

Parker had the uneasy feeling he was being set up for something. "Ennis doesn't deny he was at the scene. He got stuck in the sand there the night before the murder and had to be towed out. The garage records show that."

Gordon nodded. "You're right about it being a game of percentages. That's my problem. The forensic evidence in the Wilson case wasn't strong enough to convict Ennis. I don't know if the evidence in the Beckworth is, either. But together, they hang the sick fuck by his balls. The cases are bookends, they belong together. But I can't use one of the bookends and all my books are going to fall down. I want to make sure this animal doesn't walk. I want to make sure he doesn't kill any more teenage girls."

"I still don't see where all this is leading," Parker insisted. "You have to convince a jury, not me—"

Gordon jabbed a finger at him. "I want to convince you first. *Then* I'll convince a jury." He pushed the envelope toward Parker. "Read that. I won't even insult your intelligence by telling you what to look for."

Parker turned up his hands. "So I read it. Then what?"

The prosecutor shrugged. "Then we'll talk again."

"You expect a lot for a piece of swordfish."

Gordon grinned. "So next time, order the rack of lamb."

The car phone was ringing when Parker got back to his black BMW. It was his partner, Mike Steenbargen. "I'm at the office. When will you be in?"

Parker checked his watch. Twelve forty-five. "Ten minutes. What's up?"

"There is a lady attorney here. She says she wants to hire us, but she insists on talking to you."

"What is it about?"

"I don't know. She won't tell me."

"Did you explain to her that you're my partner?" Parker asked.

"Sure I did," Steenbargen said patiently. "She still insists on talking to you."

Parker sighed. "Why?"

"She won't say."

Just what I need, Parker thought. Another mystery. As if he didn't have enough of them.

Two

PARKER PULLED THE 633 Csi into his parking space behind the three-story, gray stone office building on Olympic that housed the new offices of Forensic Investigations, Inc.

The suite of offices consisted of a small reception area, two inner offices for the two partners, and a tiny, basically equipped lab set up mostly for the preservation and microscopic analysis of tissue samples. It was a far cry from the sophisticated lab he had been accustomed to as chief coroner, but it was also a vast improvement over what they had started with a little over a year ago, when he and Steenbargen had resigned their civil-service positions.

For the first eight months of its existence, Forensic Investigations' business address had been Parker's Hollywood Hills home, with the garage serving as lab and, occasionally, autopsy room. Their start had not been auspicious, most prospective clients balking at the $250 per hour the two partners had set as their standard rate. Parker managed to stay afloat only by teaching pathology at USC Medical Center, while Steenbargen had been forced to moonlight as an investigator for criminal attorneys in order to make ends meet. They had seriously considered folding the business and taking the tax loss when a case fell into their laps that turned things around.

It had started with a phone call from a city councilman in Charleston, South Carolina, whose son had apparently killed himself by putting a 12-gauge Remington pump-action shotgun in his mouth and pulling the trigger. The son had a cocaine problem and had been hanging around with some very bad company, and the father was dissatisfied with the local coroner's verdict of suicide. He had heard of Parker's flamboyant exploits as chief coroner of L.A., and wanted Forensic Investigations to render a second opinion.

Parker and Steenbargen agreed to take the case and flew to South Carolina. After going over the coroner's report, Parker concluded that the autopsy that had been performed on the boy had been competent and thorough—as far as it went. Toxicology analysis was negative, and no other injury that could have caused death was turned up. What had not been exhaustively explored, however, was the possibility that the shotgun blast had been used to cover up some other kind of injury. The devastation to the boy's head had been massive; an entire section of the top of the skull was missing, as well as most of the brain. Parker decided to employ a CAT scan to provide a clearer picture of the injury.

In essence, what the CAT scan did was x-ray the skull in latitudinal sections and reassemble them into a three-dimensional image. But whereas the normal CAT scan sliced the human skull into sections two millimeters thick, Parker doubled the detail, making the X-ray slices one millimeter thick. The resulting picture demonstrated that unlike the rest of the bone fragments, which had been blown outward from the shotgun blast, a portion of the frontal area of the skull above the right eye orbit showed significant indentation and fracture. Parker concluded that the indentation was the result of a blow to the head with a heavy object, and that the deceased had either been dead or unconscious when the shotgun was inserted in his mouth.

While Parker had been reconstructing the boy's death, Mike Steenbargen had been busy resurrecting the last events of his life. He discovered that the night before the boy's death, he had gotten into an altercation with a cocaine dealer over an unpaid $8,000 drug debt. In light of the new evidence, Charleston police picked up an accomplice of the drug dealer, who broke down under questioning and implicated the dealer as the murderer.

From the local media, the story was picked up by the wire services. Then *People* ran a feature piece on Forensic Investigations, calling it "the true court of last resort," and labeling the pair "Batman and Robin of the dead," an epithet that unfortunately stuck.

Suddenly, the firm could not handle all the requests for help. Letters from distressed parents, wives, husbands, pleading with Parker to right the wrongs they were all sure had been perpetrated on their loved ones by inept pathologists and an uncaring legal system. Requests from personal injury attorneys wanting Parker to back up their claims of negligence against reckless individuals and callused corporations.

After much deliberation, Parker and Steenbargen reached the mutual decision that instead of trying to expand to handle the exponentially growing volume of petitions, they would stay a two-man operation and restrict their caseload, taking on only those cases that interested them and they felt had merit. Even with that, they were still behind, often buried with paperwork, poring over letters, autopsy reports, toxicology reports, and medical histories.

On the elevator ride up to the third floor, Parker wondered about the woman waiting in the office. She was undoubtedly convinced that her case was one of those that had merit. Get in line, lady; they *all* thought they had merit. They all claimed they wanted to know the truth, but the reality was that most of them already knew it and were searching for something else. To preserve lost memories or avoid confronting their own personal failures. They wanted seventeen-year-old drug-addict hooker daughters to be the fourteen-year-old cheerleaders they cherished in their family albums, or suicidal sons to be the murder victims of someone other than themselves. Sometimes they were, but not often.

Parker stepped off the elevator and walked down to the doors of his office. Lucille smiled at him as he entered. "Good morning." She was an almost pretty thirty-year-old redhead who wore too much makeup, and stiff hairstyles that were at least ten years out of date. She was also a very efficient receptionist and secretary who kept Parker's life, at least around the office, half-sane. "Mike is in your office with a client."

"She isn't a client yet," Parker said. "Any other messages?"

She handed him two slips. "An attorney named Stein

from Chicago. He wants to know if you've gone over the material he sent. And a request to present a paper at the American Academy of Forensic Sciences convention in June."

He put the slips in his pocket and went into his office.

Steenbargen had apparently heard Parker come in and greeted him as he opened the door. He was dressed to the teeth, as usual, in a dark blue suit, crisp white shirt and paisley tie, and dark blue Oxford Loafers. With his manicured fingernails and neatly trimmed gray mustache, the man looked more like a prosperous banker than someone who had spent most of his life sifting over dead bodies in search of clues.

Steenbargen's penchant for natty attire usually contrasted sharply with Parker's preference for more casual, comfortable togs, and with his brown corduroy jacket, pale blue shirt and striped tie, khaki slacks, and brown Hush Puppies, today was no exception. Botany "500" meets Hang Ten. "Eric," Steenbargen said, smiling broadly. "This is Leah Wechsler."

The woman rose from the chair and offered her hand. She was in her late thirties, tall, and quite attractive, in an austere, outdoorsy kind of way. Her sun-streaked brown hair was pulled back and fixed in a bun, and her tanned face was devoid of makeup or other adornment. She had a wide, rather masculine jaw, a wide, thin-lipped mouth, and large brown eyes etched at the corners by a fine network of weather-lines. Her gray, pin-striped suit was tailored and accentuated the slimness of her willowy body. Her grip was firm and cool.

"I've heard a lot about you," she said, smiling vaguely.

Parker smiled back. "Good things, I hope. Please sit down." Parker went behind his desk, and when everyone was seated, began: "Mike tells me you're an attorney."

"Yes."

"Criminal?"

She shook her head. "Real estate, mostly."

Parker nodded. "What can we do for you?"

"I would like to hire you to investigate a death."

"Whose?"

"My mother's."

"When did she die?"

"Four days ago."

"I'm sorry," Parker said sincerely.

"Thank you," she said stiffly. Her manner was totally composed, her face calmly masklike. But beneath the surface, Parker could detect an unmistakable tension, especially around the corners of the mouth.

She swung the attaché case on the floor beside her chair onto her lap and flipped open the clasps. She pulled out a piece of paper from the case and handed it across the desk to Parker. It was a photostat of a death certificate.

While Parker looked it over, she said: "As you can see, the cause of death is listed as heart failure and pneumonia. Eight days ago, I visited her at Havenhurst—that's the convalescent home where she died. She was in good health. Well, relatively. Anyway, she had no symptoms of pneumonia at that time. And she had no history of heart disease."

The doctor's signature on the certificate was an illegible scrawl. Parker looked up at Leah Wechsler and said: "She was under a doctor's care?"

"An internist named Dan Katsilometes," she said. There was an unmistakable negative undertone at the mention of the name. "He treats most of the residents at Havenhurst."

"You have reason to doubt his diagnosis?"

"The man is an incompetent. He is currently embroiled in several malpractice suits involving the deaths of his patients."

"And you think this is another one of those cases?"

"That's what I'd like you to find out."

"Has an autopsy been done?" Steenbargen interjected.

She turned slightly in her chair to face him obliquely. "No."

"As next of kin, you can legally request one be done."

"That's the problem. Legally, I'm not next of kin. My brother, Bruce, is. He has—and had—power of attorney over all my mother's affairs."

"And he opposes an autopsy?" Steenbargen asked.

"Adamantly," she said.

Parker tugged on his lower lip thoughtfully. "Have you talked to Katsilometes?"

Her mouth tightened angrily. "Briefly. When I tried to ask him some questions, he turned hostile and told me that all the pertinent information was on the death certificate."

"How long had your mother been in the convalescent home?"

"A year."

"How old was she?"

"Sixty-six."

"Any other serious health problems?"

"Alzheimer's," she replied, unblinking.

Parker nodded. "Pneumonia is a common complication of Alzheimer's."

Leah Wechsler leaned forward assertively. "If my mother died of pneumonia, why won't anybody talk to me about it? The nurse who was taking care of my mother—Selma Barnes—became visibly upset when I tried to question her about that night. The administrator, Mr. Jameson, stonewalls. They're covering up something."

Parker sighed and rubbed the back of his neck. He could see how the woman's manner could become abrasive when supercharged by an event as emotional as the death of her mother. Combine that with the fact that she was an attorney with a possible negligence suit in her eyes, it was not surprising that those directly involved would be reluctant to talk. "Where is the convalescent home located?"

"Mission Viejo."

Parker glanced at Steenbargen, who had a skeptical look on his face. "The Orange County Coroner has jurisdiction in all nursing home deaths, Ms. Wechsler. If you seriously think that the circumstances of your mother's death are suspicious, and you have any evidence to back up your assertions, he is empowered to order an autopsy over the objections of your brother."

She bit her lip and shook her head. "The chief deputy coroner, Ray Thompson, won't act without the consent of my brother, and he isn't likely to get that. You see, my brother holds some rather eccentric beliefs. He always has. The particular ideas have changed over the years, but their eccentricity has always remained constant, from dabblings with Scientology to flying saucer encounter groups. Most of the groups were harmless enough, but a year or so ago, he fell in with some unscrupulous people." She paused. "Do you know much about cryonics, Dr. Parker?"

"The freezing of the dead for the purpose of future revival?"

"Yes."

Parker shrugged. "Not much. Only that there are some people who are willing to spend the money to have it done, on the gamble that medical technology will have advanced enough to be able to thaw them and cure whatever killed them. It had a minor vogue back in the seventies."

"It's alive and well," the woman said resentfully. "My brother is a passionate believer. He has been for the past two years, ever since he joined a cryonics society called Freeze Time—the brainchild of a man named Jeremy Gabriel."

Parker shook his head. "Pardon me, but what does all this have to do with your mother?"

"Bruce claims that my mother was also a believer in cryonics and wished herself to be put into cryonic suspension. He has papers she allegedly signed to that effect."

Parker blinked uncertainly. "Are you saying she's already frozen?"

Her expression remained flat, emotionless, but her voice was full of cold fury. "Not *her,*" she said, staring at Parker almost challengingly. "Her head."

Parker and Steenbargen looked at each other and the woman went on: "It's a procedure they call neuropreservation. They have fancy scientific-sounding names for everything to make it more palatable for their followers. The head is removed from the body and placed in a container filled with liquid nitrogen."

"What could they possibly think they'd be able to do with just a head?" Steenbargen asked, flabbergasted.

"Gabriel preaches that in the future science will be able to not only cure fatal diseases and reverse aging, but it will be able to clone whole new bodies from just the head of a person. It's totally absurd, of course. Just razzle-dazzle to sucker in the marks."

Steenbargen asked: "How did your mother get involved in it—through your brother?"

She turned and looked at him. Her eyes were icy. "I don't think my mother *was* involved in it. I never heard her mention the word cryonics. She didn't even know what it was. She didn't even know who *I* was the last few months of her life."

"Are you saying that her signature on those documents was forged?"

"No. The investigator I hired to look into my mother's financial affairs had the signature checked by an expert. It's hers, all right. What I'm saying is that because of advanced senility, she couldn't have known *what* she was signing. In her condition, my brother could have put anything in front of her and she would have put her name on it."

"That would be legal grounds for overturning the agreement," Steenbargen said.

"It's not that easy. The documents are dated over a year ago, when my mother was still lucid. My brother swears the date on the contract is correct and that mother was in control of all her mental faculties at the time. Gabriel has witnesses to the signing. And the doctor who was treating her at the time says that at that stage her judgment would not have been impaired by the Alzheimer's. But that's where I may get them."

She opened the attaché case and pulled out a legal-size document and showed it to Steenbargen. "This is a copy of a $300,000 irrevocable inter vivos trust agreement my mother allegedly set up six months before she died, with Freeze Time as the beneficiary. Freeze Time requires all its members to provide funds for their suspension when they sign up. They won't accept an arrangement where any portion of the procedure cost is provided by a will, because wills can be broken. They prefer life insurance policies, with Freeze Time named as the beneficiary, or trust agreements like this, because the arrangement can't be challenged later by disgruntled relatives. But such financial arrangements are part of the *signing-up* process, to ensure that the costs will be covered in case the client dies suddenly."

Steenbargen saw where she was heading. "So why would this Gabriel allow your mother six months to pay up?"

Her head bobbed triumphantly. "Exactly."

"Have you asked him?" Parker inquired.

"Gabriel won't talk to me," she said. "He has a thing about attorneys, if they're not his own."

"What about your brother? What does he say?"

"That the money was tied up in Time Deposit CDs, and that there would be substantial penalties if it was pulled out early."

"You think he's lying?"

She sighed and ran two fingers across her brow. "I don't know, but I intend to find out. I find it terribly coincidental that at the same time she allegedly set up the trust with

Freeze Time, she also had a new will drawn up, in which I am virtually disinherited. The money my brother is using to freeze mother's body was supposed to be mine."

Steenbargen and Parker exchanged significant looks. Parker asked her: "I take it you and your brother don't get along."

"No. We never have, even as children. Bruce was always terribly jealous of me. I was his main rival for mother's attentions. But there was more to it than that. Bruce was always a strange kid. He never got along well with his peers, had trouble making friends. Consequently, he grew up in his own little world, living in the refuge of his own imagination. Mother, unfortunately, encouraged it. It was a way of keeping him home, close to her. As a result, he never really matured. Bruce was always my mother's baby. She was his whole world, his whole sense of approval. He was forty-one and still living with her when he put her in the home." She looked from one to the other. "That's what this is about, don't you see? It's for Bruce to keep her alive in his mind."

"How about you?" Parker asked. "Were you and your mother close?"

Her eyes dropped. "No. I was always independent. A rebel. That made for a constant clash of wills between my mother and myself. I got out of the house as soon as I could and we grew so far apart . . . there was a terrible gulf between us. During the past eight years, I think we'd spoken on the phone only a few times. On Christmas and birthdays, mostly." She took a deep breath and her eyes took on a faraway glaze. "I regret that now. I didn't even know she was in a home until three months ago. I hardly recognized her when I saw her. I remembered her as being so strong, dynamic. The person I saw was like some mummified, mindless husk." Her eyes snapped back into focus and she said: "That's a big reason Bruce has fallen for Gabriel's scam. Gabriel claims future technology will be able to restore mother to life as she was *before* she got sick. It's all so absurd, it's hard to imagine how anyone could fall for it."

"Rationality has never been a condition for the acceptance of a screwball idea, Ms. Wechsler," Parker said. "Otherwise, fruitcake religions wouldn't be flourishing." He locked his fingers and peered over them at her. "What exactly do you want us to do, Ms. Wechsler?"

She fastened her gaze on Parker's. "I want you to find out how my mother died. I don't have to tell you the kinds of things that go on in nursing homes—the neglect and abuse."

"Did you see any evidence of that when you visited her?"

"No. But that doesn't mean anything. I was only there a few times, briefly."

"Why is your brother so opposed to an autopsy?" Parker asked.

"You'd have to ask him," she said bitterly. "Or his guru, Gabriel."

"Why would Gabriel oppose an autopsy?"

"I don't know. I don't even know if he does. All I know is that my brother doesn't make a move without consulting the man. He talks about him like he's some sort of god." She thought a moment and asked: "Might an autopsy prove whether her disease had progressed to the point that she could not have possibly been able to make rational decisions, even six months ago?"

"That would be conjecture, based on the normal pathological course of the disease," Parker said. "With Alzheimer's the variations from case to case are great. Anyway, we would most likely need the head to make any sort of determination, and I'm sure Mr. Gabriel would have strong objections to that."

"Will you take the case?" she asked.

Parker cleared his throat. "As my partner explained, Ms. Wechsler, we're currently very overburdened—"

"Please," she said, rocking forward in her chair. "You're my last hope."

Parker had to admit he was intrigued. The situation was something new, different. "You said something about forty-eight hours—"

"The Orange County Coroner is holding my mother's body and has given me forty-eight hours to come up with something that would constitute reasonable cause for him to order an autopsy. After that, he will release her body for cremation."

That swung it for Parker. Two days wouldn't set them back that far. He glanced at Steenbargen, who was stroking his mustache thoughtfully. Their eyes met and the two men nodded at each other, almost imperceptibly.

"Our rates are $250 an hour, plus expenses," Steenbargen said. "Five thousand dollars, if we have to testify in court. And we require a $5,000 retainer."

"The cost is less important than the time element."

"We'll do our best," Parker said.

Her eyes widened excitedly. "Then you'll take it?"

"Yes. With the understanding that we will spend forty-eight hours on it. If we get no results by that time, you're on your own."

"If you get no results by that time, it won't matter," she said. She took out another card and wrote something on the back. She handed it to Parker. "That's my home number. You can reach me there after seven."

Parker put it on the desk without looking at it. "We'll also want to talk to your brother—"

"When he finds out you're working for me, I doubt he'll talk with you, but you can try. His address is 415 Lucerne. His home number is 555-9088. You can reach him there most of the day."

"He doesn't work?"

She smiled sadly. "He tried to go into business for himself once. Selling bomb shelters. He blew a nice chunk of mother's money on that one. And my investigator's preliminary efforts indicate that mother herself had lost a lot of money in unwise investments in recent years—made, I'm sure, with Bruce's counsel. So she probably was more than content to let him do nothing."

"You're sure there isn't going to be a conflict of interest, you hiring two investigators to work on this?"

"Harry is just looking into mother's estate, trying to determine exactly how much money there is and where it is. He won't get in your way."

Parker nodded, satisfied, and stood up. "If you'll go with Mike, he will take care of the contractual details. He'll probably also want to ask you a few more questions. I'll be in touch."

They shook hands and she followed Steenbargen out.

Parker stared at the closed door for a moment. Leah Wechsler—a new puzzle. Free of the pressure she was experiencing, might she come across as softer, more feminine? She was obviously bright. And quick.

He flipped through his Rolodex looking for the number of the Orange County Coroner. He wondered about his decision as he put through the call. What was his *real* reason for taking on this one? The case . . . or the woman who brought it?

Three

RAY THOMPSON ANSWERED THE phone sounding surprisingly chipper for a man—he was going to mention it any moment now, Parker thought—up to his ass in alligators. "Eric, how the hell are you?"

"Good, Ray. How about you?"

"Up to my ass in alligators," the chief deputy coroner said. "You know how that goes."

Parker knew how that went, all right. He had heard that Thompson was under the gun lately, that there was political pressure building calling for his replacement. Unlike the medical examiner system in L.A. County, in which the coroner was required to be a trained forensic pathologist, the chief deputy coroner was hand-picked by the popularly elected sheriff and had to have no medical training. Thompson, who had been a coroner's investigator for twelve years, first with L.A., where Parker had first gotten to know him, then with Orange County, had been selected to head the Coroner's Division five years ago by the popular incumbent, Sheriff Del Lambert. So far, to his credit, Lambert had hung tough and had refused to bow to those voices calling for Thompson's resignation. But one more incident like the two that had occurred almost on top of each other a few months back, and Lambert would have no choice.

In L.A. the doctors were all on the county payroll, but the sheriff-coroner system in Orange County contracted its autopsies out to a private medical group, which was paid by the job. Recently, one of the group's doctors had been caught supplementing his income by removing the corpses' pituitary glands and selling them to a chemical company. Thompson fired him immediately, but not before the local papers had had a field day with the story.

The public reaction hardly had time to die down when, several weeks later, the media made another startling revelation. One of Thompson's morgue attendants had mixed up identification tags on a couple of bodies, resulting in the wrong one being released for cremation. To make matters worse, the crematee had been a likely homicide victim scheduled for autopsy, thus permanently closing the Orange County Sheriff's case.

Those sorts of screw-ups happened occasionally in any coroner's operation (more often than the public could have guessed), and although part of the blame had to lie directly at Thompson's feet, part of it also had to be blamed on the system. But since it was a hell of a lot more convenient for the politicians to single out one man than revamp the system, Thompson had predictably been designated public whipping boy.

"How's private practice?" Thompson asked.

The almost wistful undertone made Parker wonder if the question was something more than merely conversational. "Busy, Ray. Busier now, in fact, which is why I'm calling. I just took on a new client. Leah Wechsler."

"Ah."

"Would you care to amplify on that?"

"What's to amplify?"

"She says you've given her forty-eight hours to come up with grounds for an autopsy."

"That's right."

"Can you fill me in a little on the case?"

"Nothing much to fill in, Eric. The woman died under a doctor's care. The doctor was present at the time of death."

"Leah Wechsler claims there's a serious question about the doctor's competence."

"That's her story."

"It's not true?"

"I wouldn't know. Rating doctors isn't my job." Thompson took a breath and shifted the receiver to the other shoulder. "I know where you're headed, Eric, but in this case there just isn't any reason to question the cause of death. The nurse who took care of the woman, the administrator of the home, and Bruce Wechsler all back up the doctor's story."

"What about the nursing home?" Parker asked. "What kind of operation is it?"

"Top of the line."

"You have no doubts whatsoever that the woman died of natural causes?"

"There's nothing to indicate otherwise."

"Then why did you agree to hold up release of the body for forty-eight hours?"

"As a courtesy to the daughter. She has filed a request for an autopsy. I've told her that our investigation is over, I can't agree to the request, but if she turns up something tangible within that time frame, I would consider it." Thompson paused, then said: "Just between you and me, I hope she does."

"Why is that?"

"Because her brother is a jerk, for one thing. He calls up at least three times a day, trying to push his weight around. And I don't have any use for that Freeze Time bunch, either. I've had some problems with them in the past."

Parker's curiosity stirred. "What kind of problems?"

Thompson said in a peeved tone: "They think they can do whatever the hell they want, that's what. The pisser is that they seem to be getting away with it."

"Like what?"

"Like last year, for instance, they notified me they were flying in the body of a man from Texas for freezing who had died of AIDS. Not knowing much about cryonics or the procedures they used, whether or not they posed a health threat to the community, I told the head of the outfit—Gabriel—to hold up on the freezing until I could check things out, and I notified the health department to hold up a burial permit. Two days later, I found out that he'd gone ahead and frozen the guy, anyway."

Parker frowned at the phone. "That's illegal."

"That's what I told the D.A.," Thompson said. "I wanted him to file misdemeanor charges against Freeze Time on the grounds that they weren't licensed by the health department to store human remains. He turned me down."

"Why?" Parker asked, astonished.

"He didn't think he had a chance of winning. There was a similar case in Riverside a few years ago. The coroner there went after a cryonics outfit like Freeze Time on similar grounds. As you know, California law only recognizes three methods for disposing of human remains—burial, cremation, and donation for scientific purposes. Cryonic suspension doesn't fall under any of them. The lawyer for the outfit argued that just because cryonic suspension isn't listed as an option on a burial permit, it isn't necessarily illegal. The judge agreed and threw it out."

"You're telling me the coroner's office is powerless to do anything?"

"Not powerless," Thompson said. "If a death was suspicious, I'd step in in two seconds. The problem is that there aren't any laws on the books to deal with cryonics, it's such a new field."

Parker was beginning to better understand Leah Wechsler's frustration with legal loopholes.

"These people play on that," Thompson continued. "Freeze Time calls itself a medical facility, but that's bullshit. It's a place where dead bodies are interred. But by giving themselves that label, they save the million-dollar bond they'd have to put up with the state to be licensed as a cemetery. And they don't have the Cemetery Board coming in to inspect their operation and audit their books. That's something Gabriel is paranoid about. He runs his organization like a clandestine CIA operation. He won't let anyone in to see what's going on inside. Security around the place is really tight."

"You haven't been inside?" Parker asked.

"I don't know anybody who has, outside of the people who work there."

Parker mulled that over and asked: "What's the brother's objection to an autopsy?"

"I don't really know, but he has threatened to sue the county if I order one done on his mother. And that's one thing I need like another mother-in-law. You must have heard about the body mix-up we had down here?"

"Yeah."

"Well, it's snowballed," the beleaguered coroner said with a sigh. "The relatives of the cremated girl have filed a two-million-dollar lawsuit against me and the county, on the grounds their daughter's civil rights were violated. Yesterday, I got word that the relatives of the other woman are getting ready to file a personal injury suit, claiming they were traumatized by having to experience their daughter's cremation twice. I don't have to tell you, the board of supervisors is not happy about it. Several members have been putting pressure on Del Lambert to shit-can me. Another lawsuit, especially one like this, which would draw the media like a swarm of killer bees, and I'll be asking you for a job."

Parker understood the kind of pressure the man was operating under and he empathized with him. In the past, he and the jolly, bearded Thompson had engaged in numerous hot debates about the merits of the medical examiner versus the sheriff-coroner system. But in spite of Parker's personal bias that *all* coroner's systems should be controlled and administered by medical personnel, he had to admit that the Coroner's Division in Orange County was, for the most part, run with an extraordinarily high degree of efficiency. It was too bad that would not count for much when weighed against political expediency.

"You will move, though, if I can give you grounds?" Parker asked, trying to clarify the man's position.

"Bring me something strong enough and I'll move," Thompson assured him. "Just do me a favor and make it *real* strong. I've about had my quota of controversy this year."

They said their goodbyes and Parker hung up, remembering how it was to be on the hot seat, and not missing it a bit.

Steenbargen walked through the door of the office, waving a check and grinning. "How sweet it is," he said in his best Jackie Gleason imitation.

"Everything squared away?" Parker asked.

Steenbargen sat on the couch and crossed his legs. "Contracts are signed and filed. If the check is good, we're ready to move."

Parker nodded slowly and stared at his partner. "What do you think?"

"About her or the case?"

"Both."

Steenbargen shrugged. "She's pissed off, but that's understandable. If someone in my family took away my inheritance and used it to cut my mother's head off, I'd be pissed off, too."

Parker nodded. "What about the case?"

Steenbargen shrugged again. "Hard to know at this stage. Like I said, she's pissed off."

Parker leaned back and hooked his hands behind his head. "I just got off the phone with Ray Thompson. He says there's nothing to contraindicate death by natural causes, but he'll order an autopsy if we come up with something. He'd love it if we turned up something on Freeze Time. Apparently, he locked horns with Gabriel last year and lost. I think he'd like to get even."

"I investigated a case for the county back in the seventies," Steenbargen recalled. "A cryonics outfit like this Freeze Time got indicted for fraud. The owners were using the money they were supposed to be spending on liquid nitrogen to buy cars and cocaine. Their so-called patients wound up thawing out and rotting in a mausoleum in the valley. The relatives were awarded a million-dollar settlement."

"Just because one cryonics company was a fraud, it doesn't mean they all are. And you can't tell someone how to spend their money, no matter how kooky their ideas may sound."

"True," Steenbargen agreed. "But that sort of operation would be a natural con. The stakes are high, expectations for success are low, and grief makes for an easy mark. Especially a guy who's been in the bomb-shelter business."

Parker unhooked his hands and put them on the desk. "Maybe you should head on down to Orange County and see what you can dig up, since we don't have much time on this thing. Thompson said his investigators talked to the people at the nursing home, but you might double-check. And see what you can find out about Katsilometes' malpractice suits. He practices in Orange County, so they'll probably be filed there."

Steenbargen nodded and stood up. "On the way, I'll stop by the bank, just to make sure this check is good."

Parker grinned. "You are a suspicious bastard."

"Always, when it comes to money."

"I'll do what I can from this end," Parker told him. "It won't be much today, I'm afraid. I have my class at four."

"It doesn't seem quite fair," Steenbargen lamented, "that I have to slog through papers and deal with drooling convalescent home patients while you get to flirt with luscious, young female medical students—"

Parker shrugged. "Whoever said life was fair?"

"What are you lecturing on today?"

Parker stared at him poker-faced. "The joys of necrophilia."

Steenbargen nodded knowingly. "After nineteen years of marriage, I've gotten to know them well."

Four

THE WILSHIRE AREA OF Los Angeles had been settled back in the twenties and thirties by serious money, and a lot of the money was still around. The homes were old and big and Bruce Wechsler's was no exception. It was a stately Tudor-revival structure, half timber and half red brick, with a tile roof anchored on each end by a massive brick chimney.

Parker walked by the black Jaguar XJ convertible parked in the circular driveway, to the front door, and rang the bell. After a few moments the door opened a crack. The man who stared out at Parker was short and had thinning brown hair. His face was very round and he had a soft, pouty mouth and no chin to speak of. His brown eyes were weak and small. He was wearing a green and maroon Argyle sweater, dark green slacks, and black Loafers.

"Bruce Wechsler?" Parker asked.

"Yes?"

"My name is Dr. Eric Parker." He took out a card and handed it to Wechsler. "I'm a forensic pathologist. I'm sorry to intrude on your grief. I know it must be a difficult time for you, but I would like to talk to you about your mother's case, if you could spare me a moment."

"My mother's case?" Wechsler asked, surprised. He squinted hard at Parker. "You used to be the coroner."

"That's right."

Wechsler asked guardedly: "What about my mother's case?"

"May I come in?"

Wechsler ignored the question. He looked again at the card and his expression turned crafty. "Forensic Investigations. You're working for Leah, aren't you?"

"Yes."

"That bitch never gives up," Wechsler muttered angrily.

Parker said quickly: "I can assure you, Mr. Wechsler, I'm only interested in getting at the truth in this matter. I'm not trying to take sides in a family dispute. It would help me a great deal, and it would seem to me of benefit to you, too, if we could talk."

The man wavered for an instant, then pulled open the door. "Come in."

He showed Parker through a large entryway with a black and white tiled floor, into a huge living room with a high, beamed ceiling. The room was filled with ornate antique furniture and was dominated by the massive stone fireplace, which had been made into a kind of shrine.

Above the mantel hung a large oil portrait of a black-haired woman seated regally on a thronelike chair. She was perhaps thirty and very beautiful, with high, jutting cheekbones and dark, piercing eyes that seemed to be watching

Parker judgmentally. All along the mantel beneath the portrait were dozens of small, framed photographs interspersed with red glass votive candles. "Your mother?" Parker asked.

"Yes."

"She was very beautiful."

"Yes."

Parker stepped closer to the mantel and looked at the other pictures. They were all of the same woman at various ages, until in the last, she was barely recognizable. The hair was white and wispy, the skin withered, the fierce price was gone from the eyes, which now stared blankly. It appeared that Leah Wechsler had not been exaggerating her brother's devotion to his mother.

They sat down in chairs in front of the fireplace and Bruce Wechsler immediately launched into an emotional diatribe: "The only reason I'm talking to you, Dr. Parker, is that I've had it with Leah's lies. I don't know what line of crap she's given you, but the truth is, she is only after the money. That's all she wants and all she's ever wanted. She never cared about mother, she never did. As a child, she took perverse pleasure in upsetting mother by trying to thwart her wishes, which is what she is trying to do now. For the last eight years, mother never heard from her, until the end was near, and Leah smelled money. It wasn't hard to see through her act as the dutiful and repentant daughter. Mother saw through it, as sick as she was. That's why she cut her out of the will."

Wechsler's face had grown more florid as his outburst had continued, to the point where his face was now quite red. The bitterness of the harangue went beyond the boundaries of sibling rivalry, and Parker wondered just what was behind it. "May I ask why you are so opposed to an autopsy?"

The man's normal color returned. "Because there is no need for one. My mother was diagnosed as terminal by half a dozen doctors. She died under a doctor's care, in my presence. There is no reason why she should be mutilated further."

Parker realized that many people viewed autopsies as a mutilation of their loved ones, but he still rankled at the metaphor. "Excuse me, but how much more can she be mutilated?"

"Neuropreservation is not mutilation," Wechsler said stiffly. "It is a surgical technique that at the time was my mother's only chance of survival."

"Survival?"

Wechsler said, as if reciting a catechism: "Death is just a legal definition, Dr. Parker, not a biological state. And as you know, the legal definition of clinical death has changed drastically over the past fifty years. Is a person dead when his heart stops beating? That was accepted until just a few years ago. Is death the absence of detectable brain activity? That is the definition currently in vogue with the medical community, but we in cryonics believe that in the future that, too, will change, and that most cases of brain death will become reversible." He paused. "That is why we prefer the word 'deanimation' to the word 'death.' "

"How did you get involved with cryonics, Mr. Wechsler?"

"I read an article about Freeze Time in a magazine and I called up for some literature. When I read it, it made sense. I mean, at least these people seemed to be trying to *do something* about death; they weren't just sitting around waiting for it to happen to them. I realized it was a long shot, but it was like Jeremy says, you can't win a race if you don't enter. So I joined the society."

"You've made arrangements for yourself, too?"

Wechsler nodded assertively. "Of course. Mother and I signed up together."

"Your sister seems to think that you're being suckered. She thinks this Gabriel character is nothing but a con artist—"

Wechsler stiffened angrily. "I know what she's saying. Jeremy Gabriel is a genius, a true visionary. He is also a scrupulously honest man. He does not preach that cryonic suspension will work. In fact, at its present level of technology, he states flat out that it is unlikely that a patient in suspension will be revived. But we have every confidence that in the future the technology will catch up to the dream. For people who love life, what other choice is there? To be buried and eaten by worms? It's like Jeremy says, being frozen might sound like a stupid idea. The only one stupider is *not* to be frozen."

The gospel according to St. Gabriel. "You say your mother was alive when you got to the convalescent home?"

"Yes."

"What time was that?"

"Around eleven. Mr. Jameson, the chief administrator of Havenhurst, phoned about ten and said mother had apparently taken a turn for the worse. He said the doctor was on his way, but that she wasn't expected to make it through the night. Of course, I went right down."

"You were here—at home?"

"Yes."

"Was the doctor there when you got there?"

"No. He got there a few minutes later."

"How come it took him so long to get there? Wasn't he local?"

Wechsler glanced away. "He said he had another emergency and couldn't get away."

Parker nodded and tugged thoughtfully on his lip. "May I ask, Mr. Wechsler, why you decided to put your mother in a home so far away from here? Wouldn't it have been more convenient for you to put her somewhere closer?"

Wechsler said, unblinking: "Frankly, it probably would have. But my mother's survival was more important than my own convenience. Havenhurst was close to the facility and it came highly recommended."

"You mean Freeze Time?"

"Yes. It's of the utmost importance to begin the cryonic process as quickly as possible, to minimize cell death."

"You're satisfied that your mother had adequate medical care while she was at Havenhurst?"

"Not adequate," Wechsler said firmly. "The best."

"You were happy with Dr. Katsilometes as her doctor?"

"Entirely."

"Who was the doctor who originally diagnosed your mother as having Alzheimer's?"

"Noel Hammerman," he said without hesitation.

"In L.A.?"

"Cedars-Sinai."

Parker made a mental note of that and stood up. "Well, I won't take up any more of your time, Mr. Wechsler."

Wechsler rose, too. His voice grew thick with emotion: "My mother is all I have, Dr. Parker. Why is Leah trying to take her away from me?"

Parker cleared his throat uncomfortably. "Again, I'm sorry I had to bother you, but thanks for talking to me. Perhaps I can help expedite this whole matter."

"There is one thing that would expedite the matter," Wechsler said, his tone turning frosty.

"What's that?"

"If Leah dropped dead."

"Don't you mean, 'deanimated'?" Parker had to ask.

Wechsler's baby face remained stonily serious. "Not in her case," he said.

Five

THE BUZZ OF CONVERSATION hushed among the twenty-six surgically gowned and gloved students as Parker strolled into the operating theatre. "Good afternoon."

There was a tangle of "good afternoons," and some nervous foot-shuffling, as everyone once again fell silent. The tension was palpable as sidelong glances were thrown at the sheet-covered table in the center of the room.

Parker looked around at the young faces and was struck by the changes that had occurred over the past twenty years. When he had been a medical student, virtually all of the faces had been white and male. Now, as a result of affirmative action, changes in social perceptions, and an influx of foreign students, the faces were black, brown, and yellow, as well as white, and at least one-third female. But most of them had one thing in common—as had Parker's classmates: They didn't want to be here.

Before they could graduate and pursue whatever profitable and prestigious careers in medicine they contemplated, all second-year medical students had to take a year of pathology. By the vast majority, it was viewed as nothing more than an inescapable unpleasantness, but occasionally, there was one who got hooked as he had, and who abandoned the pursuit of skin rashes and yeast infections for the thankless quest of pathology. It gave Parker a great deal of satisfaction when that happened, to think he could be that kind of an inspiration. In fact, it was probably the primary reason he continued to teach. Parker wondered if there was one in this batch. Perhaps by the end of the day he would know.

He stepped over to the table and pulled off the sheet. There was a nervous tittering from the class and someone gasped. Parker paid no attention. It was a standard reaction. For some here, quite a few, probably, this was the closest they had ever come to death. The first personal encounter was always a bit unsettling, but they would all get over it. If they wanted to be doctors, they would have to.

Parker glanced around at the students, who were hanging back a few feet, and motioned them closer to the table. When they had closed in a bit, he turned to Carl Spengler, his resident-assistant, and asked: "What have we got?"

Spengler handed him a set of X rays and a medical report, which he began reading aloud. "What we have is the body of a twenty-four-year-old male Hispanic, who was found in a semiconscious state in an alley at six-thirty A.M. He had no identification on him, and from his manner of dress and hygiene, police assumed he was one of the homeless we hear so much about today. He was taken to USC Med Center Emergency. At that time, he was found to be slightly hypothermic, with a body temp of ninety-six-point-one. His white blood count was eight thousand, slightly above normal. His cell differentiation was as follows: segmented neutral fields, 45 percent; stab, 20 percent; lymphocytes, 23 percent; monocytes, 9 percent. Shortly after admission, his mental state progressively deteriorated, resulting in coma and death six hours later. A number of other tests were run, cultures taken, but no results are in yet. At this time, the doctors have not formed any opinion about the cause of death."

Parker looked around. "What kind of disease process would be responsible for those kinds of symptoms?"

"Pneumonia?" a male voice piped up. Parker recognized it as belonging to Richard Stoddard, a bright but cocky second-year student, who had made it a point to inform Parker in the third class session that he intended to be the highest-paid OB-GYN in the city.

Parker smiled mirthlessly at the sandy-haired student. "Not a bad guess. Let's take a look."

He pulled the X rays out of the envelope and set them up on the portable unit for viewing. The exposures showed a slight clouding at the bottom of both lungs. "Some congestion there, but I think we can safely conclude that John Doe here did not die from pneumonia." He purposely did not look at Stoddard. "That demonstrates the first rule of forensic pathology. Never guess until the evidence is in."

He stepped over to the stainless-steel stand alongside the table and slipped on a pair of surgical gloves. "Now, shall we see just what did kill him?"

He picked up a magnifying glass and began looking over the body slowly, inch by inch. With a tape, he took measurements, then jotted them down on the mimeographed outline of a human form that was part of the standard autopsy form. "There are no signs of external trauma. The man appears to have been grossly undernourished. He was right-handed."

"How do you know that?" one female student asked curiously.

"The right arm is slightly longer than the left," Parker said.

He felt the students tense as he selected a scalpel from the tray. The first four weeks of the course had been lectures and slides; this would be the first autopsy most of these students had witnessed. The corpse on the table was still a human being to them, but that would soon change. After the first cut, it would become just an intellectual puzzle to solve. At least for the good ones, it would.

He began the incision at the left shoulder, and in one quick stroke, brought the scalpel down to a point just below the sternum, then, without a pause, turned the blade downward, and continued the incision to the pubic symphysis. Another slashing stroke, from the right shoulder, joined the other incision at the sternum, laying open the body from chest to gut. The basic Y-cut completed, he picked up a set of standard tree clippers and began cutting through the cartilage of the rib cage. A collective intake of breath from the gallery competed with the sound of popping joints and tearing flesh as Parker reached into the chest cavity and pulled out the breastplate. The students stared in stunned fascination at the display of organs they had up to this time only seen in anatomical charts.

Parker worked quickly and methodically, and within a few minutes exposed the mastoid and larynx, and began removing the organs from the chest cavity, one by one. After getting the organ weights, he passed each around the room, instructing each student personally to handle it. A couple of them looked slightly queasy as they picked up a lung or the heart in their gloved hands.

"In no other medical specialty is organ weight or the sense of touch so important," Parker told them. "SSCCA. Remember those letters. Size, shape, color, consistency, architecture. Each of those characteristics can be the telling clue that will solve a medical mystery." He held up the bowl containing the liver, which he had just removed. "This liver, for instance. What does it tell you?"

The students gathered around. A very attractive brunette with large green eyes behind her horn-rimmed glasses, said: "It's cirrhotic."

Parker raised an eyebrow. "How do you know that, Ms.—"

"Franklin. For one thing, the color. It's yellow-brown when it should be red-brown. And it's enlarged."

Parker nodded, satisfied. "Good, Ms. Franklin. But let's not forget the A—architecture. Note the tiny bubbles on the surface of the liver, each about three millimeters in diameter. This man was suffering from microcondular cirrhosis. Not common in a person this young, but there it is, nevertheless." He looked around. "Anybody like to venture a guess now as to a cause of death?"

A few guessed cirrhosis, others guessed malnutrition, combined with exposure to the elements. "I still say pneumonia," Stoddard said.

Parker looked at him. "Really, Mr. Stoddard? Why is that?"

"The lungs each contained 350 cc's of fluid—"

"Hardly enough to cause death," Parker said. "No, Mr. Stoddard, I think we're going to have to look elsewhere for the reason this man expired. Any suggestions where?"

Stoddard shook his head silently.

Parker went to the head of the table and, with a scalpel, made an incision across the top of the skull, from ear to ear. A couple of more quick incisions and Parker peeled the scalp over the front of the corpse's face. With a striker saw, he cut around the top of the skull, then pulled off the cap with his gloved fingers.

As he severed the membranes that held the brain in place, he noted that the surface of the meninges was covered with creamy-looking puffs. He worked his gloved fingers around the loose organ and easily lifted it out. The creamy puffs covered the entire brain surface.

Parker looked up from the brain in the dish and asked: "Anybody like to tell me what we have here?"

"Meningitis?"

Parker nodded at the dark-haired male student who had made the postulation. "Precisely. Meningitis. A true killer. What we must determine is the primary site of the infection and whether this is tubercular or pneumococcal meningitis. From the look of it, I'd guess pneumococcal, but we'll take some swabs to make sure."

After taking pus swabs from beneath the meninges, Parker dissected the mastoid and the inner ear, but found no traces of pus. He then went in through the empty top of the skull into the sinuses and the back of the mouth, but still found nothing.

Parker pulled off his gloves. "Ironically, Mr. Stoddard

might have been partially right for the wrong reasons. In the absence of any other major site of infection, it just might be that pneumonia did kill this man. It is not uncommon for pneumococcal bacteria to migrate to the brain and spinal cord, resulting in sudden death. We'll know for sure by next week's class, when the results of those swabs are back."

Parker dismissed the class and cleaned up. He was on his way out of the Med Center, when he was stopped in the hall by Ms. Franklin, who had apparently been waiting for him. "Dr. Parker," she began shyly, "I was wondering if we, uh, well, if I could get together with you sometime and discuss my future in medicine. Since I took your course, I've been thinking about going into pathology."

"That's wonderful," Parker said, becoming aware of the supple shapeliness of her body now that it was not covered by a surgical smock.

She looked up at him and for a brief moment her eyes seemed to be flirting with him. He dismissed the thought, figuring that it was probably in his imagination. "Maybe we could get together and talk about it some evening?" she suggested.

It was definitely not in his imagination. He suddenly found himself at a loss for words.

She smiled and slipped a folded piece of paper into his hand. "Whenever you're free, give me a call. Anytime."

Parker admired the firm curve of her buttocks beneath her tight-fitting jeans as she sauntered off down the hall. Perhaps he should take one of his dates to an autopsy, if this was to be the reaction.

He opened the paper and stared at the phone number.

Who knew? Was this the prize student he had been waiting for, a future pioneer in the field of forensics? He would be remiss in his duties as a teacher if he put a damper on her enthusiasm in any way.

He refolded the paper and with a regretful sigh dropped it into a nearby trashcan.

Six

PARKER WENT HOME WONDERING if he might have handled the pretty med student differently if it had not been for his dinner date that evening with Mia Stockton. Lately, for a variety of reasons, he had felt like . . . what was the word? *Straying?* It was not something that he would consciously set out to do. But if the opportunity arose?

Maybe, Parker decided, arguing (not very successfully) that it would be somewhat akin to a scientific experiment. Would the fires burn brighter with someone else? Could he rediscover lost passions? Or had age and circumstance somehow taken him beyond that? Was passion, except for his work, to be only a vague memory?

There was, it seemed, only one way to find out—try it sometime—and the student sexpot was the most likely candidate he had encountered in a long time. He really ought to stop wondering what a beautiful and desirable young woman could possibly find of interest in someone his age. Hell, to her, he was probably more interesting than most of her contemporaries, and she might even find him still sexy. Were there pathologist groupies?

God, he hoped so. But not tonight.

As Parker pulled into his driveway, Pat Clemens was running in place on his front doorstep, his arms and knees pumping enthusiastically, which for a man of his girth made a startling picture. Fortunately, it was getting dark, sparing the neighbors the vision.

"You're late," Clemens complained between gasping breaths.

"You're early," Parker corrected, wondering why anyone would want an early start on what was obviously torture.

"Whatever. Get changed and let's hit it before I work myself out of the mood."

"Okay. But how about doing that on the sidewalk?"

"Why?"

"Because you're destroying the porch."

"Huh? Oh, sorry."

Pat Clemens was Parker's attorney and closest friend, and a year ago, he had asked Parker if he could join him on his evening runs, in an effort to shed the eighty or so excess pounds he carried around on his John Candy frame. Parker had been more than happy to help out, and so every weekday evening after work, they would jog three miles. And every weekday night, his guilt alleviated, Clemens would go home and consume a meal of five or six thousand calories and wonder why the fat wasn't melting off him like hot candle wax.

Parker had long ago stopped delivering lectures about the health hazards that came with obesity, but he had continued the running program, grateful for the company. And for a fat man, Clemens had built up surprising endurance, to the point where he no longer hindered Parker's pace.

Inside the house, the red light was blinking on his telephone message recorder. He checked to find a call from Eve. Oh, good, he thought, hesitating about returning it. Lately, every time he found a message from her, he felt a sense of dread.

Their relationship after the divorce had always been cool, but over the past year, it had turned frigidly hostile. Eve had always blamed Parker for the breakup of their marriage, insisting that he had been more married to his work than to her, and he had been willing to accept that, recognizing a good deal of truth in the observation.

But lately, she had taken to blaming him for everything that was wrong with her life, from money problems to her inability to sustain a lasting relationship with a man to her tendency to overeat. Whenever he would call or come to pick up Ricky for his monthly weekend visit, Eve would never miss an opportunity to remark bitterly how she had "wasted her best years" on their marriage, or bring up some selfish crime in the distant past that Parker did not even remember. (Another sign of his total self-centeredness.) Whenever Parker tried to suggest to her that she was in the throes of a mid-life crisis and that she should seek counseling, she effectively terminated discussion by going into a rage.

The event that seemed to have triggered her crisis was the dumping she had received from her boyfriend, Matt Brautigan. She had not come right out and said so, but Parker knew she had marriage designs on Brautigan, and that she had been confident that he would ask her. It had been a shock when he'd told her he was breaking off their relationship, and a double-shock when she had found out that the reason was a shapely blond fifteen years her junior. Eve had not been able to restrain her anger around the advertising agency where she worked, which was unfortunate, because Brautigan was president of the agency. After one snit too many, she had found herself unemployed, a fact for which she seemed to somehow hold Parker responsible, also.

The thing Parker feared most was that the enmity she felt for him would poison his relationship with his son. The last few weekends they had been together, Ricky had seemed a bit withdrawn, uncomfortable. Parker wondered what she had been telling Ricky about him. He wanted to ask, but he'd been afraid to, thinking that it might only exacerbate the problem. He didn't want to give Ricky the thought that he was trying to denigrate his mother: That would only perpetuate the hostilities. Better that he should work it out himself; any other way, a short-term gain could turn into a long-term loss. He picked up the phone.

"Hello?" Eve answered.

"It's me. You rang?"

She said coldly: "I just called to tell you not to bother to pick up Ricky this weekend."

"Why not?"

"Mother has had a relapse. I have to go to Palm Springs and I'm taking Ricky."

"Why are you taking Ricky?" Parker demanded curtly.

"Because I don't know when I'll be back."

Games. She had been playing them more and more. "Relapse of what? I didn't realize her last phantom illness was ever diagnosed."

She said nothing, but Parker could hear her angry

breath close to the phone. He was starting to get hot himself. "Funny how these bouts always seem to hit on my weekends."

"What is that supposed to mean?"

"Oh, come off it, Eve. You know very well you're just using Ricky as a pawn to get at me—"

"I don't have to listen to this," she said shrilly.

Parker's voice raised automatically. "I'm the one who doesn't have to listen to this. According to the court settlement, I get Ricky one weekend a month. Three out of the past six months, you've come up with some excuse why I couldn't have him—either he had a cold or your mother's mysterious illness or you had to go out of town—"

"That's just the way it is," she cut him off. "You don't like it, I suggest you take it up with your attorney."

Parker was listening to a dialtone. He dialed the number again and let it ring for a full minute before he gave up and slammed down the receiver. He stood there for a moment, trying to regain his composure, then went into the bedroom and slipped into a pair of sweats, actually looking forward to the evening's jog. He could run off his anger. And perhaps get some sage advice at the same time.

Clemens was still jogging in place on the sidewalk when Parker came out of the house. The attorney was jiggling so much, he looked like a blurred picture. They took off down the hill and covered half a mile in silence before Clemens remarked on it. "You're awfully quiet tonight."

"I have to do something about Eve," Parker said.

"What's the problem now?"

"Who the hell knows? Menopausal psychosis."

Parker laid it out and Clemens said: "She's been on

the warpath ever since she took you to court last year to get the child support payments raised."

"Maybe we shouldn't have fought it."

Clemens made a blowing sound, like a whale coming up for air. "We went all over that. You couldn't have afforded what she was asking for. The money wasn't for Ricky; we proved that. She was in debt only because of lavish personal expenditures she'd been financing on her credit cards—"

"Yeah, yeah, I know."

They reached the bottom of the hill and turned up the street that wound back around behind the house. "Hell Hill of the Damned," Clemens called it. His breathing became more labored. "She's only using Ricky to get at you. Face it. The woman flat out doesn't like you."

"I know," Parker said, the hill starting to burn his quadriceps. "And I can't figure out why. What did I ever do to her?"

"If you listen to her, nothing," Clemens gasped. "You did nothing to her or for her or with her. You ignored her completely for your work. You were self-centered, thoughtless, stingy, ill-tempered, and mean. Traits you still exhibit, I might add."

Pat had handled Parker's divorce eight years before, which was how the two had become friends, and had been a first-hand witness to Eve's acrimony. "Thanks. Nothing like a little moral support from a friend to round off the day." Mercifully, they reached the top of the grade and turned onto the street that ran along the side of the hill. Hollywood lay below, shrouded by an opaque smoggy soup. "What can I do about it?"

"That depends on what you want to do about it," Clemens said. "You can take her to court. She's abrogating your rights, according to the terms of the divorce. Of course, she'd just claim it was all on the level, that she can't help it if she has a sick mother. We'd have to prove her mother really isn't sick, which would entail putting an investigator on it. That would cost money and in all likelihood just make her madder. She'd just find some other way to screw with you."

"What do I do?" Parker asked, frustrated. "Just sit on my ass and take whatever she dishes out? Wait until my son turns eighteen before I get to see him? By that time, she'll have poisoned his mind so thoroughly, he probably won't even *want* to see me."

"So what do you do?" Clemens asked, turning the question back. "Are you asking me as your attorney or as your friend? Legal question or friend-question?"

Parker glanced at him. "There's a difference? Why, am I going to get a bill?"

"There's a difference," the attorney said, huffing laboriously. "And maybe that's your problem. You don't know the difference."

"What the hell is that supposed to mean?" Parker demanded, surprised by the hard edge in his friend's tone. It was unusual for Clemens to fault him on anything.

"Later. Right now, all I can think about is getting back to the house before I drop dead."

They finished the run in silence. Back at the house, Parker stretched out his Achilles tendons, while Clemens pressed two fingers to the side of his neck and concentrated on the second hand of his wristwatch. After ten seconds or so, he gave up. "I don't know," the lawyer lamented. "It's supposed to be a hundred and twenty, but I can never feel it."

Parker did his part: "I'm sure that beneath the fat, it's a hundred and twenty."

"Undoubtedly," Clemens said seriously.

Parker was going to let Clemens's earlier remark slide, then changed his mind. "What did you mean back there? That's my trouble—I don't know the difference?"

Clemens's fat face clouded. "What I'm trying to say," he began, obviously having difficulty, "is that at this stage, what you have isn't a legal problem at all. It's a *human* problem, and I often wonder why you can't see that. You, Eve, Rick, you're three human beings and you're the ones who have to work it out."

Parker protested: "How am I going to do that? She's such a bitch!"

"Granted. But there's no law against that. And therefore no legal solution."

"So?"

"So, solve it yourself," Clemens said with finality. "Quit asking society—or me—to solve it for you. You have a personal problem? Look inside yourself."

"Hey," Parker said, stung by the rebuke, "I was just asking a little advice of a friend."

"Once too often," Clemens told him. "We've been 'round and 'round on this one, buddy, and frankly, it's getting boring. You say Rick is the most important thing in your life, yet you can't seem to find a way to make him a part of your life. You can't blame all that on Eve. That's bullshit and you know it."

Parker stared at him, stunned. Normally, the man was

totally supportive, and when he did offer criticism, his fat man's legendary sense of humor went a long way toward softening the blow. But there was no humor now in his friend's manner.

"You're so goddamn smart," Clemens said, shrugging. "Be inventive."

Seven

PARKER ARRIVED AT VALENTINO'S ten minutes early and decided to do his time at the bar. He was sipping his second glass of Chardonnay when Mia Stockton arrived, twenty minutes late, which was pretty prompt for Mia.

Parker wasn't the only one who had noticed her entrance. In spite of the fact that her blond hair was tucked up under a black felt fedora and that her curvaceous figure was hidden beneath a long, baggy-sleeved gray overcoat, she was instantly recognizable and a subject of scrutiny for more than one turned head in the room. The unfortunate price of television stardom in a society that worshipped its celebrities.

They had met as a result of Parker's last case as chief coroner for the county—the murder of actor-comedian John Duffy, Mia's one-time series costar and one-time lover. Parker had found himself incredibly attracted to her, an attraction she claimed was mutual, and since that time, a little over a year ago, they had been dating steadily. Or as steadily as you could date with the kinds of schedules they both kept.

They often half-joked that their schedules were probably why things had worked out so well so far between them. One of the reasons Parker's marriage had disintegrated (at least according to Eve) was Parker's prolonged absences, but with Mia's hectic shooting schedule, that kind of pressure was absent from their relationship. They never had the chance to get on each other's nerves, and the time they did spend together was always fresh and new, a time of romance and discovery—or at least it had been, that is, until recently. Now?

Now, it was going flat, Parker thought, and if he had to say why, it was, incongruously, because of the same things that made it so good. While not seeing each other very often kept things fresh and new for them, they were without firm foundation, drifting on a kind of romantic Jell-O.

And that was not likely to change. They were both acutely aware that their careers came first, and neither was anxious to ruin things by trying to push the other into making any kind of commitment.

There was another reason Parker didn't push things with Mia. To be truthful with himself, he was not really sure how he felt about her. He was still dazzled by her sexiness, her honesty, and her intelligence, and although he liked her a great deal, he was not sure if he loved her. In some ways, he had to admit to himself that he was afraid to find out. The bitterness of his divorce had left him gun-shy.

"Hello, darling," she said, and kissed him lightly on

the mouth. "Sorry I'm late. Shooting ran over. The Jock couldn't remember his lines again. I swear, all those smacking helmets must have jarred something loose."

"The Jock" was Bubba Harris, a four-time Pro Bowl defensive end for the New York Giants, and now Mia's costar in "Our Happy Home," a new half-hour sitcom about a stewardess who hires a retired football player to take care of her three kids while she flies around the country. It was not very original, not very funny, and according to the ratings, the public loved it.

"I need a drink," she said, and pulled off her coat. Beneath it, she was wearing a gray pin-striped jumpsuit with wide lapels. On another woman, it might have looked masculine, but not on her.

Parker had often tried unsuccessfully to analyze what made Mia so damned attractive. Taken one at a time, her features were actually almost gross. True, she had great eyes—huge and long-lashed and startlingly blue. But her nose was too big, her chin was too pointed, and she had a noticeable Gene Tierney overbite. But somehow, all the flaws came together into a compelling gestalt, and on the screen the transformation was astounding. The change was not just due to the miracles of makeup; Mia was one of those people whom the camera loved.

Parker signaled the bartender over and Mia said tensely: "I've about had it with this crap. It's the same thing every day. It's just damned lucky we're not shooting in front of a live audience. It's actually painful to watch. The amazing thing is that Bubba is actually beginning to think he's *good*! He was at least tolerable when he started, before the ratings started to go up. He was just a puffed-up jerk. Now, he's an insufferable puffed-up jerk."

Parker shook his head sympathetically. "The crosses we must bear for a hit series and $25,000 a week."

"Go ahead, make fun," she snapped. "You don't have to listen to the people you work with."

The bartender arrived and smiled profusely at Mia. "Good evening, Miss Stockton. This is a real pleasure. I wouldn't miss your show."

"Thanks," she said, graciously returning the smile. "I'll have a vodka martini, please."

"Coming right up." He shook his head and chuckled. "Tell Bubba hello for me. He cracks me up. My whole family loves him."

The smile froze on her face. "Make that a double."

Parker tried, but was unable to suppress a grin, which seemed to make her even madder.

The bartender returned with the drink as the maitre d' came over to tell them the table Parker had requested against the back wall was ready. There was no way to completely avoid the inevitable stares and occasional autograph seeker with cocktail napkin in hand; all one could do was try to protect one's flanks from attack.

Settled at the table, Mia decided on the scampi and Parker chose the veal scallopini Marsala, both with Caesar salads to start. To go with the dinner Parker ordered a bottle of Robert Mondavi fumé blanc.

"How's Ricky?" Mia asked, sipping her wine.

Parker shrugged. "Fine, I guess."

"You haven't talked to him?"

"Not this week. Eve is playing games again."

"Now what?" Mia demanded, frowning.

Parker gave another small shrug.

"There must have been something that set her off,"

Mia persisted. "That seems to be one of her few good traits. Right or wrong, she always has a reason."

"Maybe she's jealous," Parker said, toying with his wine glass, not sure where he was going. His talk with Clemens—and the reprimand that came with it—was still fresh in his mind.

"Jealous? Of what?"

"You. Us."

Mia raised a quizzical eyebrow. "What makes you think that?"

"Oh, I don't know. Little remarks she drops about the 'TV bimbo.' "

"This is a new development," Mia said mildly. "When did it start?"

Parker looked at her, surprised by the subdued, matter-of-fact reaction. He had expected anger and he still wasn't sure why he had tried to provoke it. "I guess Ricky talks you up a lot at home. You're a big source of prestige for him among his friends at school."

She hesitated and her eyes clouded for a moment. "Surely she knows I only want what she wants—whatever is best for the boy."

Her voice was thick with sincerity. Parker knew she meant that. In the beginning of their relationship, it had never occurred to Parker that however limited the contact, Mia would begin to feel deeply about Rick. But at some undefined point, months back, that had obviously happened.

"Maybe she feels threatened by you," he said.

"Threatened?"

"Ricky is all she has."

"Maybe I should talk to her."

Parker shook his head, but he realized, with some measure of guilt, that this was what he had been maneuvering for from the beginning of the conversation. Despite Clemens's lecture, he still wasn't up to the job. He still needed a proxy to fight the most important battle of his life.

Mia said, "I think I can make her understand that what she has is special, inviolate, and that I respect that. I—*we*—just bring in another dimension, that's all. We're important to Ricky and he does need us, but we'll always be secondary. I'm sure I can show her that."

"And I can't?"

Her tone took on an acerbic edge. "You obviously haven't so far."

That was true, Parker had to admit. He also had to admit that Mia and Ricky had a special relationship that grew out of Mia's innate understanding of children. Her understanding was much greater than Parker's, even with his own son. Parker had tried to analyze it—that was one of his major faults, Mia often told him, trying to analyze everything—and had decided that it probably had a lot to do with what made her a good actress. The ability to suspend disbelief, to fantasize and conjure emotion at will was shared by actors and children.

"It can't hurt," she went on. "I mean, it can't get any worse. You two have been at each other's throats since the divorce. You want to damage each other, and Ricky is the one who is suffering for it. I don't want to be used in that way. Let me talk to her."

Parker was not sure it would do any good, but certainly she was right about his own failure. He was spending four days a month simply trying to counter a propaganda campaign Eve waged the other twenty-six. It was madness. "Okay," he said gratefully.

"I'll call her tomorrow."

The dinner arrived and they whiled away the next hour and a half savoring the food and each other's company. The drinks and wine left them both feeling mellow. Finally, Parker was moved to ask the eternal question. "Want to mess around?"

She smiled. "Not tonight."

He looked at her, surprised. "That's not the kind of answer a bimbo is supposed to give. Bimbos are supposed to be pushovers."

"I'm a special type," she said. "Working bimbo. I have to be up at five-thirty."

He lifted one corner of his mouth, and sat back. "How about this weekend? We can go over to Catalina."

"Sounds like fun," she said agreeably. "But isn't this your weekend with Ricky?"

"Eve is taking him out of town."

"Then, sure. I'd love to go."

He paid the check and they went outside. The attendant brought up her silver Carrera and Parker kissed her goodnight and watched her drive off.

What the hell, Parker thought, experiencing mixed emotions. A trip to Catalina, baking in the sun and relaxing with Mia, sounded inviting, but he felt a pang of guilt about giving up his weekend with Ricky so easily. He shrugged. More combat at this stage was not going to help matters. Better to wait and see how the conversation between Mia and Eve went. That would be best, he told himself. That would be easiest.

Eight

IT WAS AFTER ELEVEN when Parker closed the folder on the desk and rubbed his tired eyes. He got up and made himself a drink and went out the sliding glass door onto the deck.

The night air was cool, damp. He sipped his drink and stared out at the seemingly infinite grid of smoldering color below. He had purchased the tiny two-bedroom house above Hollywood shortly after his divorce. It was vastly overpriced at a time when he could hardly afford it, but he had found the place irresistible. Rather, he had found the view irresistible. On those nights when the events of the day crowded in on him, he could step out onto his porch and somehow the lights soothed, calmed him. But tonight the magic wasn't working. His troubled thoughts refused to be calmed.

For most people, reports like the one he'd left on his desk would be a dull recitation of dry, abstruse facts, but for Parker it was a drama as tragic and inexorable as if it were being played out on a stage in front of him. The actors were there, the tragedy, the violence, all culminating in pain and death. In this particular drama, the villain had walked away and the ingenue had died horribly. Gordon was right about the two cases—they were bookends. More correctly, the jaws of a vise that closed on Lamar Ennis.

An analysis of the semen found in the vaginal tract of Sally Beckworth, Ennis's latest alleged victim, determined that the murderer was an ABO Type A secretor, with a genetic marker of PGM 2 + 2, which put him in a category that included fourteen percent of the male Caucasian population. The tests for GLO type were inconclusive, as GLO correlations are labile when mixed with vaginal secretions, and since the sample had been used up conducting the standard test, there was none left for DNA analysis.

But in the case of Jeanette Wilson, the case on the desk, the killer had also left a sample of semen on the dead girl's panties, providing a specimen uncontaminated by other body fluids. An analysis came up with GLO I, which matched Ennis's. The GLO type, in combination with the other genetic markers in the Beckworth case, considerably narrowed the percentages. Unfortunately, the amount of the specimen was so small that it was completely used up before PGM tests could be run, thus precluding that correlation from being made.

But the most compelling evidence was the pattern injury found on the scalp of the Wilson girl, on the occipital area behind the right ear. The injury, which consisted of eight circular contusions, each .05 cm in diameter, with uninvolved areas of scalp between, was thought at first by the pathologist to be ringworm, but that question was settled by the presence of galeal hemorrhage adjacent to the injury, confirming that it had been traumatically induced.

To get a clear picture of the pattern, the pathologist

had overlaid acetate paper on the wound and traced the pattern with a marking pen. When he had finished, he had a series of alternating circles and squares.

Although there was no speculation in the report as to what had caused the injury, Parker knew what it was. He had seen that pattern before, in the police crime scene reports on the Beckworth murder. It was a pattern that had been found on the ground near the murder site and on the soles of a pair of boots found in the back of Ennis's van. At some point during his several-hours-long celebration of torture, Ennis had stomped on the poor terrified teenager's head, indelibly embossing her scalp with the Mark of the Beast.

There was no doubt in Parker's mind that Ennis had killed both girls. The question was, what could he do about it. He was a scientist. All he could do in court was answer questions about the facts, and the Beckworth jury would never be allowed to hear the facts of the Wilson case.

He could call Sheldon Roth, Ennis's attorney, and tell him he was convinced Ennis was guilty and return his $5,000 fee for testifying. Technically, Roth could still subpoena him to testify, but the attorney would not want to risk putting Parker on the stand at that point, knowing his opinion of his client's guilt. That would relieve Parker of the personal obligation of contributing to Ennis's defense, but it probably wouldn't matter as far as the outcome of the case was concerned. Roth would just hire another forensic expert to testify in Parker's place.

It all came down to semantical games, all of his work. Most people would think that performing an autopsy was the most unpleasant part of a forensic pathologist's job, but at least in the autopsy room there were finalities, solutions. Parker had spent a lifetime trying to dispel ambiguities, only to have attorneys try to use his words to create them, to befuddle. Lamar Ennis was an animal who belonged on death row, and Roth was going to try to make Parker open the cell door so that he could go out and kill again.

What was it all for? What the hell had he done with his life? Maybe Eve had been right. Maybe he should have become a psychiatrist, applying useless unguents to neuroses, or a plastic surgeon, inflating bosoms and tucking tummies for incredible sums. Perhaps then he would still have had a wife and son from whom he was now becoming more alienated with each passing week. At least he would have been spreading some happiness among the living. Instead, he had spent his life working for a civil servant's pay in stench-filled rooms, taking apart the remnants of others' sad lives, quantifying their failures and worries in terms of enlarged hearts and fatty livers.

Somebody had to do it, right? Right. But why him? Because there had been no choice. His interest in forensic pathology had been sparked in his teen years, when his father's reputation as a physician had been saved by a pathologist's scalpel. In medical school, pathology had only been a dreaded requirement for most students, but Parker had been hooked from his first autopsy. It had been the investigative aspect of forensic work that had fascinated him, the intellectual exercise of piecing together the events that had led to the final denouement of death. That fascination, coupled ironically with his own ambition, which drove him compulsively to be the best at whatever he did, had pulled him in. In forensics, he had seen a wide-open field, in which a man with talent and imagination could rise rapidly to the top.

He proved his vision to be true, and within ten years, Parker had gained an international reputation. He *had* made a difference—at least he liked to think he had—pioneering new techniques, challenging the frontiers of the science with bold and innovative suggestions. He was proud of his accomplishments, and it was only at odd times like this that he questioned his original decision. It was odd, he thought, that a piece of human garbage like Lamar Ennis could be the one to make him do it.

Parker's thoughts were interrupted by the ringing of the phone. He went inside and picked up the living room extension.

"Did I wake you?" Steenbargen asked.

"No. What's up?"

"Not a hell of a lot. Jameson, the administrator at Havenhurst, was out of town today. I made an appointment with him for nine-thirty tomorrow morning. I did talk to the nurse who took care of June Wechsler. Selma Barnes. She was pretty busy and couldn't talk much—or wouldn't. What she did say pretty much backs up death by natural causes."

"What do you mean by 'wouldn't'?"

"I don't know. It was the way she acted. The minute I mentioned the Wechsler case, she started acting real nervous. She kept looking around, as if she expected someone to come barging in on us at any moment. She answered a couple of questions, then said she had an urgent case to attend to, but I had the feeling she just wanted to get away."

Parker chewed that one over, then asked: "Did you talk to Katsilometes?"

"Nix. I didn't have time. But I did get some of the details on his two malpractice suits. One was filed by a woman whose husband went to Katsilometes to check out some chest pains he was having. Katsilometes ran an EKG, told the guy nothing was wrong, and sent him home. He died a few hours later of a myocardial infarction."

"Nice."

"The other one is even better. Also filed by a widow, Mrs. Ellen McNulty of Costa Mesa. Seems her husband was a longtime patient of Katsilometes and went to see him about some joint pain he'd been having in his shoulder. Katsilometes diagnosed it as arthritis and prescribed prednisone. Turns out the guy had been treated for TB while he'd been in the army in Korea back in the early fifties. Four weeks after he started taking the steroids, he was admitted to the hospital with disseminated TB and died."

"No doctor with half a brain would prescribe steroids to someone with a history of TB," Parker said, astonished. "He'd have to know they would reactivate the disease."

"His widow agrees with you. Strangely enough, so does Katsilometes. He claims the man never told him he'd had TB, and there is no mention of it in the man's medical history. I talked to the widow this afternoon. She claims Katsilometes is lying, that her husband told her before he died that it was in his records, and that Katsilometes knew all about it."

"What is she saying, that the medical history was changed?"

"That's what she's saying."

"Interesting," Parker said, his mind working over the possibilities.

"I thought so. So did a friend of mine with the Medical Quality Assurance Board. He told me they've looked into several other complaints about Katsilometes, but could never find enough to warrant yanking his license."

Parker said: "I'll meet you at Havenhurst tomorrow morning. I'd like to be there for your meeting with Jameson."

Steenbargen gave him directions for the convalescent home, then told him that if he needed him for anything, he was at the Saddleback Inn in Santa Ana. Parker told him to book him a room there for the next night, then hung up and went back into the den.

He stared for a moment at the report on the desk, then went to the bookshelves that lined one wall. He ran his hand along the bindings until he found the title he wanted, an old book by the nineteenth-century French medicolegalist P. C. H. Brouardel. He flipped it open to the bookmarked page and read: "If the law has made you a witness, remain a man of science. You have no victim to avenge, no guilty or innocent person to convict or save—you must bear testimony within the limits of science."

Usually, when he faced this sort of dilemma, reading that passage over made him feel better. But not tonight, for some reason. Tonight, it would have to be another drink and Letterman. He made himself one, turned out the lights, and went into the bedroom.

Nine

TWENTY SHORT YEARS AGO, Orange County had been a wide-open area of rolling, grass-covered hills and agricultural acreage, its air sweet with the smell of citrus. Since the suburban stampede of the late sixties, however, things had changed considerably. The smell of automobile exhaust had replaced the perfume of orange blossoms, and the hills that had not been leveled were covered with outrageously overpriced condominiums and townhouses, which all looked as if they had been scissored from the same ugly template. In another year or two, Parker figured, the transformation would be complete. Every square mile of unused land would be built up and the Yuppie Dream would come to full realization—fifty square miles of malls, shopping centers, supermarkets, gas stations, and fast-food eateries, all connected by a network of freeways that were too congested to use for twenty-two of the twenty-four hours.

Mission Viejo was one of those new Orange County communities that had sprouted in all their radiant, stuccoed splendor, almost overnight. They all had Spanish-sounding names and were all done in the same boring pseudo-Mexican architectural style.

Havenhurst Convalescent Home fit right in with the city's master plan. It was a large, rambling one-story building with a swirled stucco exterior and a terra-cotta tile roof. Steenbargen was waiting in the lot as Parker pulled in and parked, and the two of them went inside.

As in most convalescent homes, the hallways were filled with the ghostly whisperings of shuffling slippered feet and the smells of disappointment and death. Parker had seen a lot worse in his time, however. At least the floors were clean, the nursing staff seemed to be fairly efficient, and none of the residents he saw on the way to the administrator's office looked as if they were getting their last meal from a cat food can.

Arthur Jameson turned out to be a thin-faced man with a red toupee that lay on his head like a dead animal. The man with him, perhaps twenty years his junior, had his own hair but looked dead himself. He had the bulging eyes and dry flaked skin of an expired fish.

"This is William Barnaby," Jameson said by way of introduction. "He is the attorney for Havenhurst. I thought it appropriate that he sit in."

Barnaby made no move to rise or offer any kind of salutation. Parker nodded and moved into the closest empty chair. Steenbargen waited a moment, then sat down next to Barnaby.

Parker began: "There is really no need—"

"Mr. Jameson isn't interested in your opinion," Barnaby cut him off. "He is interested in mine, which is why I'm here."

"I really don't see what Miss Wechsler is trying to accomplish with all this," Jameson said in an exasperated tone. "The cause of her mother's death has been established. There was a physician present. The care at Havenhurst is second to none. What exactly is she trying to prove?"

"She isn't trying to *prove* anything," Parker replied. "She just has some questions in her mind about her mother's death that she would like answered. I'm sure you can understand that."

"Frankly, I can't," Jameson said, steepling his fingers. "I've answered all her questions honestly and she is apparently still dissatisfied. I can only conclude that she thinks I am lying for some reason."

Parker tried to calm the man down: "Nobody thinks you're lying, Mr. Jameson. The woman is just upset by the loss of her mother. Your cooperation can help her through this trying time." Before the man had a chance to respond to that, Parker asked: "How long had Mrs. Wechsler had pneumonia?"

Jameson shifted in his chair and stuck out his lips. He thought for a moment, then said grudgingly: "About a week, I suppose."

"And she was being treated for it by Dr. Katsilometes?"

"Yes."

"Why wasn't she taken to a hospital?"

"She didn't wish to be," Jameson said. "When she came to us, she specifically instructed that no heroic measures should be taken to keep her alive. She knew she was going to die here. That was what she wanted. Our job was to keep her as comfortable as possible, and that was what we did."

"She was lucid enough to make that decision?" Steenbargen asked.

"At that time, yes."

"Did you ever hear her talk about cryonics?"

"Often."

"During her lucid period?"

"Yes."

"Then she was aware she was going to be frozen?"

Jameson seemed surprised by the question. "Of course. I was present when she signed the papers."

"What do you think of Gabriel and his operation?"

Jameson shrugged. "I think he is a sincere man. He believes in what he is doing. So did June Wechsler, which is all that matters."

"Leah Wechsler says her mother never mentioned cryonics during the times she visited her—"

"I don't doubt that," Jameson said acidly. "June Wechsler was at Havenhurst for a year. During that time, her daughter visited her perhaps half a dozen times, all during the last three months of her life. By that time, the Alzheimer's was in the advanced stage. Half the time, the woman didn't know where she was."

"Were you present when Mrs. Wechsler died?"

"No," he said, glancing away. "I didn't see any need for it. There was nothing I could do. It was a medical emergency."

"You were notified, then?"

"Certainly. Miss Barnes phoned me around ten and told me Mrs. Wechsler was experiencing severe chest pains. She suspected that she had had a coronary event and had notified Dr. Katsilometes. I immediately phoned Bruce Wechsler and Freeze Time, as per my instructions."

"What time did the doctor arrive?"

Barnaby interrupted before Jameson could answer. "That is a question more properly put to the doctor."

"I was just—"

"If you have doctor-questions, ask the doctor," Barnaby said, his dead fisheyes bulging.

"What about nurse-questions?" Steenbargen asked.

Barnaby made an empty motion that seemed to translate into "nothing changed."

"What room was she in?" Parker asked, starting over.

"One sixty-two." Jameson paused and eyed Parker obliquely. "Why do you ask?"

"Just curious," Parker replied, and before Jameson could give the question more thought, asked: "Who removed the body?"

"Mr. Gabriel and his team."

Steenbargen wrote the information down on his pad. "What time was that?"

"I really don't know. Some time after midnight. I'm told that's when she died."

"Does Dr. Katsilometes take care of a lot of the patients here?" Parker asked.

"Quite a few."

"You'd rate him as a competent doctor?"

Jameson's face acquired a patina of irritation. "Very. I am aware of your client's aspersions on Dr. Katsilometes' professional reputation, Dr. Parker, and I must say I find them personally insulting. They reflect not only on Dr. Katsilometes, who is a thorough and caring physician, but on the entire staff at Havenhurst. To be frank, Dr. Parker, the only thing suspicious about June Wechsler's death is her daughter's motive for hiring you."

Parker shook his head. "I'm not sure I follow you."

Jameson's expression turned world-weary. "We see this sort of thing here all the time. Relatives who never cared about their mother or father while they were alive suddenly come out of the woodwork, pointing fingers, threatening legal action. It's the money, Dr. Parker. It makes people do and say strange things."

"You're suggesting Leah Wechsler has done something strange?" Parker asked.

"He's suggesting nothing of the sort," Barnaby interjected. "The reference was to people in general." He stood up with an effort. "Mr. Jameson has given you a full account of what he knows. I don't see any reason for this to continue." The smile belonged to a corpse. "Have a nice day."

Parker exchanged glances with Steenbargen. "If that's how you feel." He paused, then managed to get the words out. "Thanks for your time."

In the hall, Steenbargen asked: "What do you think?"

Parker shrugged. "I don't know. It seems a little odd to have an attorney present at this stage."

"Like maybe Jameson is afraid of a lawsuit?"

Parker shrugged. "Let's talk to the nurse."

"She works the night shift," Steenbargen said. "Doesn't come on until four."

"You have her address?"

Steenbargen took a toothpick out of his coat pocket and stuck it into the corner of his mouth. "What do you think I've been doing down here? Sticking my dick in the mud?"

Parker grinned. "We'll drop over for a visit, but first, I want to check something out."

The door to Room 161 was open, but Parker knocked before walking in. The room was small and white and clean, the bed looked freshly made, its blue blanket tucked neatly beneath its mattress. There was a small writing desk in the corner and a big sunflower that had been scissored out of red paper was scotch-taped to the wall over it. By the window, soaking up the sunlight that fell in a warm rectangle around the room's lone chair, sat a wasted, sunken-cheeked man, dressed in a blue terrycloth bathrobe, which, unlike the bed, did not look as if it had been changed in a while. A few wisps of white hair stuck to his scalp stubbornly, like strands of fine cotton candy.

"Hello," Parker said.

For the first time, the man became aware of the presence of strangers, and turned his liver-spotted face toward them. "Who are you?" he asked weakly.

"My name is Dr. Parker. This is Mike. What's your name?"

"Chaney. Peter Chaney." The watery eyes narrowed suspiciously. "What do you want? I don't need no doctor."

"I'm not here to treat you, Mr. Chaney. I just want to ask you a few questions, if you feel up to it."

"Why wouldn't I feel up to it?" the old man asked belligerently. "I'm not sick." The eyes remained wary. "What kind of questions?"

"Did you know the woman next door? Mrs. Wechsler?"

Chaney ran a blue-veined hand over his barren skull. "They came for her the other night." He added slowly: "They always come late at night."

"Who always comes late at night, Mr. Chaney?"

Chaney scowled. "The angels of death."

Parker and Steenbargen exchanged knowing glances.

Chaney's scowl turned suddenly into a sly grin. "They come here all the time. They think they're gonna get me, but they won't. Not until I'm ready." He pulled a sharpened pencil out of the pocket of his robe. "They think they're going to take me before I'm ready, they're gonna get a big surprise."

The old man waved the pencil around, fending off the pack of imaginary assailants. It was apparent the man was not firing on all eight plugs.

"These angels of death, the ones who took away Mrs. Wechsler," Parker asked. "You've seen them here before?"

The old man's brow furrowed and he looked at them as if they were the ones who were crazy. "Sure. Lots of times. Always late at night. I don't sleep so good."

Chaney stuck the pencil back into his pocket quickly as a smiling nurse in a starched pink uniform rolled a wheelchair through the door. "Time for physical therapy, Mr. Chaney—" She broke off when she saw Parker and Steenbargen. "Oh. I didn't realize Mr. Chaney had company."

"We were just leaving," Steenbargen told her.

Her manner turned apologetic: "I don't mean to run you off. Mr. Chaney doesn't get many visitors. Are you relatives?"

Steenbargen nodded. "Distant cousins."

Parker smiled. "He was telling us about Mrs. Wechsler next door."

She nodded sadly. "Poor woman. She passed on a couple of nights ago."

Parker studied her face for a reaction. "He says that the same people who came for her come around here quite often."

Her eyes widened cannily. "The angels of death?"

"Yes."

She nodded indulgently. "They are one of Mr. Chaney's favorite subjects."

Parker leaned toward her and whispered: "You mean, it's all in his imagination?"

"I'm afraid so."

Chaney did not seem to be paying any more attention to them and had gone back to staring out the window.

The nurse wheeled the chair over to the window and Steenbargen helped her lift the old man into it. "He'll be through with physical therapy in an hour, if you want to visit some more," she said.

Parker made an obvious point of checking his watch. "We have to run."

"Too bad," she said as if she meant it. "He gets so few visitors."

Parker leaned toward her and whispered: "He has a sharpened pencil in his pocket. To ward off the angels."

Parker and Steenbargen slipped into the hallway as the nurse tried to cajole the Ticonderoga sword away from her charge.

"Guy was nuttier than a fruitcake," Steenbargen remarked.

"Sure," Parker agreed. "That doesn't mean he didn't see what he said he saw."

"I'm sure he did," Steenbargen said sarcastically. "Any place the average resident is over seventy and in failing health is going to keep the body-removal services pretty busy."

"That's who you think his 'angels of death' were?"

"Who else?" Steenbargen asked casually.

"You're probably right," Parker agreed, pushing open the door and stepping out into the morning sunlight. He checked his watch. Their options seemed to be running out with every advance of his minute hand. "Let's go talk to that nurse."

Ten

THE NEIGHBORHOOD IN GARDEN Grove was among those overrun by "boat people" who had poured into the area from southeast Asia in the late 1970s, and the faces that Parker and Steenbargen passed on the street were all Vietnamese and Cambodian.

Selma Barnes's address was a tiny stucco tract home that looked exactly like all the rest on the street, except that its front lawn was dying and its need of paint was more desperate. A brown, two-year-old Hyundai with a dented right front fender stood in the driveway.

Two small Vietnamese girls in the front yard of the house next door stopped playing to watch Parker and Steenbargen get out of their car and start up the cracked concrete walk toward the front door of 762. Parker waved and smiled. The girls hid their faces and giggled.

The door was answered by a slim, middle-aged woman dressed in a plaid wool bathrobe and pink house slippers. Her short, dark hair was tousled, and her eyes looked sleepy. They lost their sleepy look when they lighted on Steenbargen. She pulled the lapels of her robe across her chest protectively and snapped: "What are you doing here? How did you get my address?"

"The phone book," Steenbargen said. "Sorry to bother you this early, Miss Barnes, but—"

"What do you want?" she cut him off.

"This is my partner, Dr. Eric Parker. We'd like to ask you a few questions—"

"What about?"

Parker studied the woman's face. It was pleasant enough, but unremarkable, the kind of face you would see once, then quickly forget. "You were on duty at the onset of June Wechsler's symptoms—"

Her eyes grew anxious and she shook her head. "You're going to have to talk to Mr. Jameson."

"We just did," Parker said.

Her grip tensed visibly on her robe and she pulled it tighter across her breasts, to the point that her fists were almost under her chin. "I'm sure I can't add anything to what he told you."

"Maybe you can," Parker pressed. "If I could just ask you a few questions—"

Her body rocked slightly back and forth as she nervously shifted her weight from one foot to the other. "I can't help you."

"Why not?" Steenbargen pressed her.

"I just can't, that's all," she said, her voice quivering with emotion. "I'm sorry. Please leave me alone."

"But Miss Barnes—" Parker tried.

"I'm sorry," she repeated and closed the door.

Parker looked at Steenbargen, who turned up his hands in a puzzled shrug. Parker knocked on the door again, but nothing happened. He took out a business card and on the back wrote down his and Steenbargen's room numbers at the Saddleback Inn. He bent down and slipped it under the door and shouted: "In case you change your mind, Miss Barnes, call one of us at any time. We'll be in town for the next two days."

He listened at the door, but there was no response.

On the way to the car, Parker waved again at the two children, but this time they did not giggle, but only stared with dark, wary eyes. After watching the encounter with Selma Barnes, they seemed to sense that the strangers were unwanted intruders in the neighborhood.

As they drove off, Parker said: "You were right about the woman being spooked."

"Yeah. I wonder what's making her so jumpy?"

Parker sighed. "Whatever it is, we'd better find out in the next twenty-four hours, or it won't matter much."

Parker called Katsilometes' office, but was informed by a churlish-sounding receptionist that Dr. Katsilometes did not take phone calls during business hours and that if Parker wanted to leave a number, she would pass on the message. Parker explained that his partner had left a message yesterday but the doctor had not called back, to which the woman replied sharply that she had no control over what the doctor did; all she could do was give him his messages. Parker gave her the number of the hotel and hung up.

"I'll hold my breath," Steenbargen said derisively.

As they swung onto the onramp of the freeway, the phone buzzed. They looked at each other and Parker picked it up.

"I figured you'd want the message," Lucille said. "A Bruce Wechsler just called. He wants you to get in touch with him immediately. He left a 714 number."

Seven-one-four was Orange County. Parker called the number and received a small jolt when a man's voice answered: "Freeze Time."

"Bruce Wechsler, please. Dr. Eric Parker calling."

"Just a moment." Parker was put on hold, then Wechsler came on the line. "Dr. Parker. Jeremy Gabriel would like to meet you. He thought you might like to take a look at his facility."

"I would like that very much."

"Where are you?"

"Orange County."

"Where?"

"Heading north on the Santa Ana Freeway." He looked out the window at the ramp signs. "Coming up to Seventeenth."

"Turn around and head south to First. Make a right to Grand and make a left to Hunt Street. It's just past the railroad tracks. The address is 38097 Hunt."

"My partner is with me."

"That's fine. Just ring the buzzer on the outside gate."

Parker was holding a dead line. He put the receiver back and Steenbargen asked: "What was that all about?"

"Wechsler is over at Freeze Time. Apparently his guru Gabriel wants to meet me. He has honored us by extending us a rare invitation inside the place."

Steenbargen raised a dubious eyebrow. "That's pretty good timing."

"Yeah," Parker said, troubled. "Too damned good."

"He doesn't mind if I tag along?"

"I have the feeling he already knew you'd be coming," Parker said uneasily.

Eleven

HUNT STREET WAS A two-block, dead-end street of grimy-looking industrial buildings in a commercial area of Santa Ana. The address number, but no name, was painted on the outside of the reinforced concrete building. The building was set back from the street and its perimeter was enclosed by a high Cyclone fence topped with barbed wire. There were two signs on the gate. One read: Ring Bell for Entry. The other said: WARNING! VICIOUS DOGS ON PREMISES.

Whatever exaggerated claims Freeze Time was making, the latter was not one of them. The two large black Rottweilers made a point of showing Parker and Steenbargen all of their teeth as they repeatedly hit the fence and barked out vociferous territorial warnings.

While they waited a couple of uncomfortable moments to see if the fence would hold, a voice came from the speaker box by the gate: "Yes?"

"Dr. Eric Parker to see Bruce Wechsler."

"Just a moment."

The dogs continued to snarl as the front door of the building opened and a man stepped out. "Damien! Shaitan! Heel!"

The dogs immediately left the fence and trotted over to the man and sat down. He was dark-complected, six three or four, and must have weighed two hundred and thirty pounds, most of it muscle. His chest and arms were putting a visible strain on his tight-fitting blue T-shirt. The electronic lock on the gate buzzed as it was released from inside the building, and the man called out: "Come in."

The eyes of the dogs never left Parker and Steenbargen as they stepped warily through the gate.

"Don't worry," the big man said, sensing their apprehension. "They won't hurt you."

Steenbargen nudged Parker as they walked toward the building and pointed to the closed-circuit camera mounted above the door.

Despite the assurances of their escort, both men felt better when they stepped inside and the door shut behind them. They were in a small, barren reception room. Another camera was mounted on the ceiling, trained on the front door. Although 1984 had come and gone without event, it seemed that at least in here, Big Brother was alive and well.

There were two doors on either side of the room. The big man moved to the one on the right and opened it with a key. They followed him up a set of stairs and down a carpeted hallway to another door. He opened this one without using a key and went in.

They entered a large gray office dominated by a huge mahogany desk. Behind the desk stood a very tall, thin man dressed in a white linen suit and purple sports shirt. The man smiled and said in a rich, mellow baritone: "Dr. Parker. This is a pleasure."

Parker was struck by the physical appearance of the man. His face was long and strikingly pale, with lineless skin as smooth and white as eggshell. Although he could not have been more than forty, his hair, which was combed straight back from his tall forehead, was snow-white. He could have been albino if it had not been for the eyes, which were pale blue. "I'm Jeremy Gabriel," he said, thrusting out a slender white hand. His grip was surprisingly strong. He waved at Bruce Wechsler, who was sitting quietly in a red leather chair in a corner of the room. He had on a long-sleeved plaid shirt and gray slacks. "You already know Bruce, of course."

Parker introduced Steenbargen and Gabriel said: "I've read all about Mr. Steenbargen. 'Batman and Robin.' You used to be chief investigator under Dr. Parker."

"That's right," Steenbargen said.

Gabriel nodded and said effusively: "This meeting is quite fortuitous. Bruce happened to be down here today and when he mentioned your meeting yesterday, I had him immediately call your office, and lo and behold, your secretary said you were in Orange County. The Fates had stepped in once again." He paused and smiled strangely. "I've followed your career with great interest over the years, and I must say, I think the county of Los Angeles acted very stupidly when they lost you. Although that is probably the only way politicians know how to act."

"Thanks," Parker said. "But the department seems to be getting along fine without me."

"That's hard to believe," Gabriel said seriously. "You

are one of the true pioneers working on the frontier of death."

Parker thought the statement strange, but said nothing. He felt oddly ill at ease and he tried to identify the source of his discomfort. Perhaps it was the intensity of Gabriel's stare, which seemed to be trying to bore holes in his face, or the smile that never reached the icy blue eyes.

Gabriel broke the spell by saying: "You can go, Reid."

The big man went out and Parker said: "He's a handy man with dogs."

"Yes," Gabriel said. "And other things. Reid is our chief of security."

"I noticed the closed-circuit equipment. You have a problem here which requires that much security?"

"It's purely precautionary," Gabriel said. "We had a couple of break-ins when we first moved in here. Valuable equipment was destroyed. A few of us have had our cars vandalized."

"You know who did it?" Steenbargen asked.

Gabriel turned his stare on the investigator. "Animal rights groups. Besides serving as a storage facility, we do research here. Some of it involves animals."

"What kind of research?" Parker asked.

"In a moment, I'll show you."

Gabriel asked them to sit on the couch across from the two red chairs, which he and Wechsler occupied. Parker took the opportunity to look around the room. Behind the desk were bookshelves filled with books with scientific-sounding titles. There was a potted ficus and areca palm, both petrified. That figured, Parker thought.

The wall behind the two chairs in which Wechsler and

Gabriel sat was lined with framed black-and-white photographs. From the ages and appearance of the men and women in the photos, they had all been taken a long time ago. Several of the smiling young men were dressed in World War II uniforms, others stood in front of 1940s cars, their arms around young women in pleated skirts and bobby sox.

Gabriel noticed Parker looking at the photographs and said: "Our patients."

"You mean the people who are stored here?"

"When they were younger, of course," Gabriel said. "We like to keep the memory of them intact that way so that their loved ones can have a vision of what they will be like after revival."

Parker nodded dumbly. He was beginning to feel as if he had wandered into a lost episode of "The Twilight Zone." "Were you present when Mrs. Wechsler died—excuse me, 'deanimated'—Mr. Gabriel?"

"Yes. Mr. Jameson called me around ten and notified me of the situation. I went immediately to the lab and got the equipment and crew ready to transport the patient."

Patient. Parker tried not to show a reaction to the terminology. "Who was there when you arrived?"

"Bruce and Dr. Katsilometes."

"How soon after you arrived did Mrs. Wechsler expire?"

"Twenty minutes, perhaps."

"And you began your process immediately?"

"Yes. Speed is of the essence in our work. Death is not a finality, but a process. Different cells die at different rates. The less deterioration and cell death, the more likely the complete revival of the personality."

"In Mrs. Wechsler's case, a senile personality," Parker said.

Gabriel's smooth demeanor remained unruffled. "We are counting on the advancement of science, particularly the development of nanotechnology—the use of molecular machines—to take care of that problem. We foresee a time when we will be able to construct bacteria that will be able to target certain tissues and carry out repair programs that are built into their DNA. The aging process itself will be reversible. We will be able to control growth and development, indeed, program types of growth that do not normally occur, such as growing an entire body from a head, regenerating brain tissue, entire vascular systems."

"You have a lot of faith in science," Parker mused.

"Science *is* my faith," Gabriel replied. "If I believed in the survival of the spirit after death and all that other religious hocus-pocus, I would never have gotten into cryonics. But I believe in man and his ability to solve problems. We in cryonics believe that everything will be accomplished that does not violate the natural laws of the universe. What we are doing, Doctor, is gambling on ourselves and the future. But without the gamble, what choice is there? To rot in the ground. There are no other options."

"That's right," Wechsler chimed in. "A few short years ago, the idea of freezing and storing human organs for transplant was science fiction. Now, it's just science."

The man's enthusiasm seemed real enough, but the words had a rehearsed sound to them. He sounded like a Moonie handing out a standardized line of patter at an airport terminal.

Gabriel broke in: "You've talked with Dr. Katsilometes?"

Parker shook his head. "Not yet. Mike tried to talk to him yesterday, but it seems the doctor is too busy to spare fifteen minutes."

Gabriel turned to Wechsler. "Maybe you should give Dr. Katsilometes a call, Bruce. Since your mother was his patient, perhaps a word from you would help convince him to spare Dr. Parker a few minutes." The way he said it, it sounded more like an order than a request.

"I'll call him," Wechsler responded like a good soldier.

Gabriel nodded and said: "Once you talk to Dr. Katsilometes, Dr. Parker, I think you'll see that Leah Wechsler's claims are totally unfounded."

The man's voice was soft, persuasive, and Parker found himself half-believing the words. Katsilometes was the man to talk to.

Gabriel stood up and said enthusiastically: "Come. We can talk further while I give you the sixty-cent tour."

He led the way out of the office and down a back stairway. At the bottom of the stairs, they went through a steel door, into a large, high-ceilinged room brightly lit with overhead fluorescents.

Parker's attention was immediately grabbed by the four gleaming stainless-steel cylinders that stood in a row in the center of the room. Two of them were ten feet tall, the other two were half as tall, and all were mounted on wheels. A series of wires ran from the tops of the cylinders to a nearby, complicated-looking control bank of gauges and dials manned by another white-coated crewcut clone of Reid. Another frocked attendant, this one a female with long brown hair, watched the bank of TV monitors on the far wall.

There were other pieces of equipment around the

room—a hospital crash cart, complete with a cardiac monitor and defibrillator, a portable heart-lung unit, and a hemodialysis machine. Bathed in the stark artificial light, which gave off a faint electrical hum, the scene had an unreal look about it, like a set from an old 1930s Frankenstein movie. Parker looked around for a hunchback, but that seemed to be one detail Gabriel had overlooked.

Parker pointed at the cylinders. "Are those the storage units?"

"Our 'Forever Flasks,' " Gabriel said. "The large units hold up to four entire bodies. The short tanks can hold four heads."

Parker wondered silently which one held June Wechsler's. "They look like giant thermos bottles."

"In a way, that's just what they are. Inside is a cylinder of stainless steel with multiple radiation barriers of aluminized Mylar. We use stainless steel because it doesn't become brittle at low temperatures. There is a vacuum space between the outer and inner skins for insulation. Even with all that, the liquid nitrogen slowly boils off and has to be replenished every few months. Those wires are hooked up to monitors that tell us when the levels are getting low. The containers also have an automatic alarm system coupled to paging beepers carried by our personnel at all times. If the nitrogen levels drop for some reason, the alarm is triggered."

"How cold is it inside?"

"Minus 196 degrees Centigrade," Gabriel said.

"Wouldn't the cells rupture at that temperature?"

"They would if the body was immersed without first going through a gradual cooling process."

"What exactly *is* the process?"

Gabriel looked pleased that Parker had asked the question. "Upon deanimation, the patient is packed in ice. At the same time, he is placed on a heart-lung resuscitator to keep the blood oxygenated and circulating, and anticoagulants and pentobarbital are administered—"

"Pentobarbital?" Parker interrupted, surprised.

Gabriel nodded. "We have found that the patient can continue to have agonal spasms up to forty minutes following cardiac arrest. The pentobarbital quiets this, as well as reducing brain damage from reduced circulation."

Parker thought that to be nonsense, but said nothing. Giving a dead person pentobarbitol would be about like giving him a high colonic. It wouldn't do anything, but it wouldn't hurt him.

Gabriel continued: "After that, the patient is packed in dry ice and transported here, where the femoral artery is surgically lifted from the groin and hooked up to a pump. The blood is pumped out and replaced with a cryoprotective solution of fifteen percent glycerol—"

"Sort of like an antifreeze," Parker observed.

"Exactly!" Gabriel exclaimed. "Most cell-damage during freezing is due to the expansion of water in the cells as it freezes. Replacement of water by glycerol prevents that. It has been known for some time that certain animals, like wood frogs and turtles, can freeze solid during the winter by producing a glucose-sugar solution and pumping it through their own bloodstreams. We've just improved on the formula."

"Fascinating," Parker said, in an effort to keep him primed.

Gabriel nodded. "After perfusion, the patient is further cooled, then gradually lowered into the tank of liquid nitrogen to await revival. The entire process takes about twelve days."

"How much does the process cost?"

"One hundred and twenty-five thousand dollars for a full body, forty thousand for neuropreservation. There are also maintenance costs. About $4,000 a year for a full body, $1,500 for a head. Those costs are provided by the interest generated by the initial deposit."

"How many 'patients' do you have stored here?"

"Eight full body and eleven neuropreservations."

"Any of them from Havenhurst? Besides Mrs. Wechsler, I mean."

Gabriel looked at him sharply. "Why do you ask that?"

Parker shrugged indifferently. "Just curious."

"All patient information is kept strictly confidential, Dr. Parker. I'm sure you can understand that."

"Mrs. Wechsler's trust fund is for $300,000. Where is the other $260,000 going?"

Gabriel waved a slender hand at a door on the other side of the room. "Come, I'll show you."

They went through the door, into a small but well-equipped operating room. Two men dressed in surgical smocks and masks stood around the operating table in the center of the room, working on an anesthetized black puppy that was packed in ice. Tubes ran from the dog's legs to a portable electric pump on a cart next to the table. The pump was working, pumping the dog's blood into bottles on the cart.

Parker glanced at Steenbargen, whose face was darkly angry as he watched the animal being drained of blood.

"Much of our money goes to research on how to minimize the damage of the freezing process. The danger to living cells is not their ability to endure storage at very low temperatures, but traversing the intermediate zone of minus fifteen to minus sixty degrees. What we're doing here is lowering the dog's temperature to ten degrees Centigrade and replacing its blood with glycerol. We keep the lungs ventilated artificially. Later, we pump the blood back into the animal and revive it, none the worse for wear. We've been able to keep cats and dogs in suspended animation for up to seven hours in that way."

"Are they normal when revived?"

"See for yourself," Gabriel said, and led them through another door.

They were immediately greeted by a piercing clamor of barking. The room was lined with cages, all filled with pacing dogs and cats. Gabriel shouted: "Most of these animals have gone through the same process as the puppy in the operating room, and as you can see, they are all okay."

The dogs seemed to be disagreeing with that observation. Their barking was shrill, pleading. Parker felt as if he had been washed up on the island of Dr. Moreau. Welcome to the House of Pain.

"We had some initial failures," Gabriel shouted over the din, "but we made some adjustments and ironed out the problem."

"What kind of failures?"

"Brain damage. An autopsy on the animals found that in some cases of ischemia, calcium becomes concentrated in the muscular walls of the brain arteries, causing cellular spasms. To prevent that, we administered Verapamil to prevent calcium infiltration, and dexamethasone to reduce brain swelling."

Parker could see why animal rights activists would

have a bone to pick with Freeze Time. It was a canine Auschwitz. "Can we get out of here?" Parker shouted uncomfortably.

They went back out through the operating room and into the lab and Parker said: "Freezing and reviving live animals is one thing. Bringing a dead one back to life is quite another—"

Gabriel dismissed the objection with a wave of his hand. "Again, where do we draw the line? The myth that the brain suffers irreversible damage after eight or ten minutes without blood has been disproved again and again. We have proved here in work with animals that the brain can be deprived of blood for at least an hour without damage. All that is needed is to raise the blood pressure to force circulation through the swollen tissues."

Parker wondered how long it would take for the rest of medical science to catch up with Gabriel's amazing discoveries.

"Where did you get your training, Mr. Gabriel?"

"The University of Wisconsin."

"Medical school?"

"Two years."

"Why didn't you become a doctor?"

For the first time, the calm surface of the blue eyes was stirred. His entire face seemed to grow taut as he said: "Financial reasons. I've always retained my interest, though, and have kept up on the literature."

"Obviously," Parker said. If his attempt at flattery was obvious, Gabriel did not let on. "What did you do before you got into cryonics?"

"I was involved in holistic medicine," he said vaguely.

"Really? In what capacity?"

"I had a small clinic that specialized in intestinal therapy."

"Intestinal therapy?"

"High colonics," Gabriel said without batting an eye. "Well? What do you think about our operation?"

"Very interesting," Parker hedged.

Gabriel obviously read more into the response. "I knew you'd think so! Your approach to forensics has always been bold. That's why I wanted to show you what we're doing. We have been dismissed by the scientific establishment as kooks and hucksters. But that's because traditionally the spokesmen for the scientific community have been afraid to be bold. They have been hampered by the weight of their own superstitious philosophy. The thought of improving the human phenotype scares the hell out of them. They condemn what we are trying to do as 'playing God,' but the fact is, if man hadn't played God in the past, we would all still be dying of smallpox."

Parker looked at him closely. "What do you mean by 'improving the human phenotype'?"

Gabriel looked faintly surprised by the question. "Why, the coming of the Superman," he said matter-of-factly.

Parker tried to maintain a blank expression. "The Superman?"

Gabriel nodded. "In the future, man will be as different from us as modern man is from the australopithecines. Presently, man is only limited by his own thinking. There is no reason why we cannot construct a man superior in every way—physically, mentally, emotionally. A being resistant to cold and heat, who can perhaps fly or breathe underwater. One who will be able to metabolize mineral nitrogen, thus reducing the need for proteins and solving the human food problem."

The man's tone was rational enough. Perhaps that was what bothered Parker more than anything. "You think you're going to be playing a part in that evolutionary jump?"

Gabriel said calmly: "A man or woman of this generation has no chance of becoming Supermen unless he or she survives until a later era."

Somehow, Parker had trouble envisioning Bruce Wechsler as a Superman.

"It's certainly refreshing in this pessimistic age to run into a group of people with such an optimistic view of mankind's future," Parker said, trying to keep any hint of sarcasm out of his voice.

Gabriel dipped his head slightly. "We in cryonics are chronic optimists. That's why I took the chance on you."

"It only takes one success to prove a pessimist wrong," Wechsler interjected, "but a thousand failures can only prove that the optimist is wrong *so far.*"

A catchy aphorism and not an original one, Parker was sure. He had little trouble guessing where Wechsler had gotten it.

Gabriel said: "We are dedicated to what we are doing because we see it as the right thing to do. We are optimistic about the future of mankind, but at the same time we realize that each one of us is responsible for his own life and survival." He paused and smiled. "Would you care to sign up, Dr. Parker? I am prepared to offer you the chance of seeing the future, on the house."

"That's a very generous offer," Parker said.

"One I am willing to back up in writing right now."

"If I accepted, I guess I would be endorsing cryonics. And, of course, you would want the right to use my name for publicity purposes—"

Gabriel shrugged nonchalantly. "It would always be helpful for a man of your scientific stature publicly to sanction our work."

"I'll think about it," Parker lied.

"Splendid," Gabriel said, obviously pleased. "May I ask what you are going to tell Leah Wechsler?"

"I want to talk to Dr. Katsilometes before I decide."

"I'm sure you will come to the right decision," Gabriel said in a condescending tone. "The woman is doomed to failure. She is spiteful and small-minded, and small-minded people cannot succeed against us."

"Do you have any written material I can take with me?" Parker asked.

Gabriel turned to Wechsler. "Bruce, get Dr. Parker an information packet. You know where they are."

The future Superman scurried off, and Parker said: "Quite a handy little errand boy."

Gabriel said reprovingly: "We function as a team at Freeze Time, Dr. Parker. Every worker does his job happily, because he knows he is investing in the future."

Wechsler a little heavier than most, Parker thought. Three hundred grand didn't buy much these days, it seemed.

Wechsler returned momentarily with a stack of pamphlets. Parker took them and said: "I really appreciate you and Mr. Wechsler taking the time to talk to us."

"Anytime," Gabriel said, then signaled to Reid, who was lurking in the doorway. "Show Dr. Parker out."

They all shook hands and Parker and Steenbargen followed Reid down a narrow concrete hallway to a door. They found themselves in the reception room, then outside, traversing the yard under the watchful eyes of the two Rottweilers.

"Traitors," Steenbargen said to the dogs as they went through the gate.

Reid turned without saying anything and went back into the building.

In the car, Steenbargen said: "I'm sure glad to be out of there. That place is fucking Weird City." He shook his head. "I can't believe he seriously thought you might endorse his nutsoid operation."

"Maybe he didn't," Parker said, starting up the BMW. "Maybe he was just testing my reaction."

"You give him that much credit?"

Parker shrugged. "Even if he's crazy, it doesn't mean he's stupid."

Steenbargen grinned broadly. "No. He has to be smart to go from giving enemas to producing the fucking Superman. You think he really believes that horseshit?"

"You wear a mask long enough and it sticks to your face. Wear it long enough and it becomes your face."

"I have to admit, the guy has the razzmatazz down. He even had me going a couple of times with the technical double-talk."

"That's one of the keys to the success of any religious cult—obscurity. Make things hard for the laity to understand and set yourself up as the only one who has the dictionary to translate it."

"He sure has Wechsler on a string," Steenbargen remarked. "Every time the guy opened his mouth, it sounded as if he was reading from a script. And it isn't hard to guess who the screenwriter was. I thought you might call him on it."

Parker backed out of the parking space and headed down the street. "I didn't want to antagonize either one of them right now. Especially Gabriel. I have a strong feeling that as long as he sees me as a possible convert—or at least not the enemy—doors will remain open for us."

"He wasn't looking at you like a possible convert when you brought up medical school."

"He was pretty touchy about that subject, wasn't he?"

Steenbargen nodded. "Speaking of doctors, what about Katsilometes?"

"Let's find out," Parker said, picking up the car phone. He dialed Katsilometes' office number. The receptionist took his name and a moment later a male voice said: "Dr. Parker, this is Dr. Katsilometes. Sorry I was tied up when you called before. I understand you'd like to talk to me about June Wechsler."

"Yes."

"If you'd like to come over now, I can spare you a few minutes." He did not sound too happy about it.

"That would be fine," Parker said, his voice dripping with false appreciation.

"I'm always willing to extend professional courtesy," Katsilometes said curtly.

Parker hung up. "Another door mysteriously opens."

"I'll say one thing, the man is prompt in delivering on his promises," Steenbargen said. "It's too bad we won't be around to see if he comes through on the Superman stuff."

"Speak for yourself," Parker said. "He offered me a freebee. I just might take him up on it."

Twelve

DR. DANIEL KATSILOMETES HAD the look of a man who made time in his busy doctor's schedule to enjoy life. His square-jawed, handsome face was deeply tanned and the corners of his dark brown eyes were etched by wind and sun from hours of sailing. His teeth were perfectly capped and very white, his jet-black hair didn't have a hint of gray, and his forty-six-year-old body was trim and fit from racquetball and weights and forty minutes of aerobics three times a week. He probably drove a Ferrari, Parker decided. Or maybe a Porsche. With a personalized license plate, of course.

He tried to smile, but the smile looked forced, tense. He fussed with some papers on his desk and said: "I'm afraid I can only give you a few minutes, Dr. Parker. I do have patients to see—"

"I understand," Parker said, thinking that was the first lie. There had been two patients and eight empty chairs in the outer office. Today might have just been a slow day, but if it was typical, the man was going to have trouble with payments on that fancy car. "You've talked to Bruce Wechsler?"

"Yes."

"Then you know we're looking into his mother's death."

"What's to look into?" Katsilometes snapped. "The woman died of natural causes."

Parker shrugged apologetically: "What can I say? Leah Wechsler has retained us. We have to . . . what? Go through the motions?"

Katsilometes' expression seemed to relax. Payment for services rendered was a concept he understood.

Parker continued: "When did you first treat Mrs. Wechsler for pneumonia?"

"Five or six days preceding her death."

"How were you treating her?"

"Antibiotics. Keflex and erythromycin."

"She didn't respond to the drugs?"

"On the contrary, she was responding quite well. But the pneumonia put an extra strain on her heart, which was already weak."

Katsilometes glanced guardedly at Steenbargen as the investigator took out his notebook and scribbled some notes. "What are you doing?"

Steenbargen shrugged innocently and smiled. "Just taking some things down." He asked pointedly: "You don't mind, do you?"

"Why should I mind?" Katsilometes said defensively.

Parker asked: "What time did you arrive at Havenhurst that night?"

Katsilometes hesitated, then scratched the side of his nose. "Around eleven-thirty."

"You were called at the same time as Bruce Wechsler and he had to come all the way from the valley—"

Katsilometes seemed to anticipate the question. "I had another emergency."

Parker paused. "What did you do for Mrs. Wechsler when you got there?"

"There was not much I could do," Katsilometes answered flatly, turning up a palm. "It was apparent she was dying, and she had left strict instructions—no heroic measures. That wish was reiterated by her son, who was there."

"You'd been Mrs. Wechsler's doctor for as long as she'd been at Havenhurst?"

"Yes."

"How advanced was her Alzheimer's when you first started treating her?"

"There was marked deterioration of her mental faculties over the past four or five months. Before that, she had long periods where she was quite lucid."

"Did she ever talk about cryonics during those lucid periods?"

"Frequently," Katsilometes said.

"Were you still there when Gabriel and his people got there?"

Katsilometes pressed two fingers to his lips. "I was just leaving."

"Had you ever met him before?"

"Who?"

"Gabriel."

Katsilometes licked his lips, touched his nose again. He looked down at the desktop. "Once, I believe."

"Where?"

"At Havenhurst."

"With Mrs. Wechsler?" Parker asked.

Katsilometes hesitated. A light film of perspiration had broken out on his forehead. "I believe so, yes."

"What do you think of cryonics, Doctor?"

Katsilometes shrugged stiffly: "However someone wants to dispose of his own remains is a personal matter."

Parker nodded and pretended to look around the paneled office. Fat medical volumes lined the shelves on the walls, a doctor's how-to manuals. "I'm assuming from your treatment of Mrs. Wechsler that her pneumonia was bacterial."

"That is correct."

"What was the basis of your diagnosis?"

"X rays and sputum and blood analysis."

"Would it be all right if I looked at the lab results and Mrs. Wechsler's medical records?"

Katsilometes' eyes narrowed warily. "I don't think so."

"Why not?" Parker asked.

Katsilometes' tone turned frigid. "Because there is no reason for it. I'm telling you what the results were. If that isn't good enough for you, I must assume that you think I'm lying for some reason."

Parker shook his head and smiled. "I can assure you, Doctor, that wasn't my meaning."

"Just what *was* your meaning?"

"With those records, I could clearly demonstrate to Ms. Wechsler that her accusations are unfounded and that she should drop the matter."

"I don't care about Miss Wechsler's accusations," Katsilometes said sharply.

Parker shrugged casually: "I just thought that it would

be in your interests, especially in view of the two malpractice suits you have pending against you—"

Katsilometes' lips compressed angrily. "Those suits are totally without basis." He hesitated, then said in a tremulous voice: "I agreed to see you because of professional courtesy and because Bruce Wechsler asked me to. I know what your client is up to, and being a doctor, I thought you of all people would understand. We are all potential targets for any shyster attorney or deadbeat relative who sees a chance to get rich quick by filing a malpractice suit."

Parker tried to get a word of appeasement in, but Katsilometes stood up abruptly. "I have patients to see, gentlemen. I've said all I'm going to say."

Steenbargen waited until they had gotten outside, then said: "Nervous fuck, isn't he?"

"He's on edge about something," Parker agreed. "Maybe he's just touchy about the fact that he has two malpractice suits against him."

"Maybe that's part of it," Steenbargen said. "But he was lying in there."

"About what?" Parker asked as they walked to the car. Katsilometes' building sat on a bluff overlooking South Laguna, and in the distance Catalina was dimly visible across the blue expanse of ocean.

Steenbargen stopped and took out the small spiral notebook in which he had been scribbling notes while Katsilometes talked. "The time he arrived at Havenhurst. And about how well he knows Gabriel."

"How do you know that?" Parker asked curiously.

Steenbargen jabbed the notebook emphatically twice, with a forefinger. "I wrote it down. 'Rubbed nose.' " He held it up for Parker to see. "See there? Twice, after 'what time Havenhurst?' and 'met Gabriel before?' "

" 'Rubbed nose'?" Parker asked, hoping for some clarification.

Steenbargen nodded. "Lying results in an increase in tension, which sets up certain physiological changes, such as dryness of the mouth and increasing sensitivity of the nasal cavities, causing the nose to itch."

Parker had to smile. "Where did you learn that?"

"Books on body language," Steenbargen said, straight-faced. "And watching doctors lie. They're usually pretty good at it; they get a lot of practice with their patients, but even they can't cover up completely."

Parker chuckled and said: "I guess that's one good thing about being a forensic pathologist. You don't have to lie to your patients."

Steenbargen smiled and opened the car door. "That's right. And one thing is for sure. They never lie to you."

Thirteen

AFTER GRABBING SOME LUNCH at a trendy seaside restaurant where the view was figured into the price of the meal, Parker drove Steenbargen to his car and followed him back to Santa Ana.

The Saddleback Inn was a rambling, two-story hotel complex that occupied both sides of First Street. Steenbargen had picked it because of its strategic location—next to the freeway and less than a mile from the Orange County offices—and because the rooms were comfortable and adequate for their work needs, with writing desks and telephones with outside lines. Parker was unpacking his overnight bag when Steenbargen knocked and stuck his head through the half-open door. "I don't know if I mentioned it, but I have to go home tonight. My wife has had tickets to this show for two months and I promised to take her."

"When will you be back?"

"Late tonight."

Parker nodded. "There isn't anything you could do around here tonight, anyway. Enjoy the show."

"Yeah," Steenbargen said sourly.

"What show is it?" Parker asked curiously.

"Pajama Game."

Parker's eyebrows raised. "Isn't that play a little dated? I mean, we have airplanes now and everything."

"Look," Steenbargen said, "this is not something I'm particularly looking forward to. But it's important to Marie. It's opening night and her favorite star is in it. She bought a new dress for the occasion and everything, and if I didn't take her I'd have to move in here permanently."

"Who's the star?"

"Van Johnson."

"Van Johnson?" Parker remarked, surprised. "He must be one hundred and four years old."

"He's making a comeback."

"At least he'll feel comfortable in the part," Parker said. "The play is from his era." He told Steenbargen he would see him in the morning, then settled down to make some calls.

Ray Thompson's secretary told him that her boss would be out for the rest of the day, but would be in around eight tomorrow morning. Parker than called L.A. information for the number of Dr. Noel Hammerman.

Hammerman was not much help. The last time he had seen June Wechsler as a patient had been some eighteen months before. At that time, her symptoms were intermittent, and her periods of senility were still of comparatively minor duration. Parker thanked him and called Leah Wechsler.

She sounded frustrated when Parker reported their progress to date. "In other words," she said irritably, "you're no closer to proving anything than yesterday."

"So far, there's nothing to prove. Everybody tells basically the same story."

"What about that nurse?"

"Something is bothering her, and she may talk about it eventually, but eventually won't help us. We need some results by tomorrow."

"So what do you intend to do?" she asked.

"I'm going to see Ray Thompson in the morning and try to talk him into ordering an autopsy over your brother's objections."

"He won't do it."

"We'll see," Parker said. Her negativity was starting to grate on him. He told her he would call her in the morning and hung up.

Parker stretched out on the bed and began going over the Freeze Time pamphlets. Most were sales pitches, talking up Freeze Time's faith in mankind and the future, interspersed with some general information about financing and legal arrangements for cryonic suspension. But a couple of the papers were more technical. One, titled, "Case Study of Patient #B-123," particularly interested Parker, and he went through it slowly.

The twenty-one-page tract, written by Gabriel, was a step-by-step account of the Freeze Time suspension procedure, as performed on a patient presumably still stored at the facility. The paper was a mishmash of technical mumbo jumbo, graphs, schematic diagrams, all laid out in the most arcane medicalese.

After reading it, Parker was convinced more than ever that Gabriel was playing doctor. The only time Gabriel had ever come close to losing his cool at the lab was when Parker had asked him about his medical background. Parker would have been willing to bet that all Gabriel had ever wanted to be was a doctor, but couldn't cut it. He made a note on the margin of the tract to check out Gabriel's records at the University of Wisconsin, then pored over the paper again. On the third read, he found the material to be not only arcane, but downright soporific.

He was startled awake by the ringing of the phone and looked bleary-eyed at his watch. Nine fifty-one. He snatched up the receiver. "Hello?"

"Dr. Parker?" The female voice sounded vaguely familiar.

"Yes?"

"This is Selma Barnes."

Parker blinked and sat up on the bed. "Yes, Ms. Barnes?"

"I have to talk to you." Her voice sounded taut, shaky. "I'll probably be fired, but I don't care. I can't lie anymore."

"About what, Ms. Barnes?"

"June Wechsler."

"What about her?"

There was a long pause. "I'm not sure she was dead when they took her away."

Parker tried to digest that. "What do you mean, you're not sure she was dead?"

"They wouldn't let me in the room."

"Who wouldn't let you in the room?"

She took a breath. "Gabriel and his people and Bruce Wechsler. When they got there, Mrs. Wechsler was still alive. They pushed me out of the room and locked the door. I called Mr. Jameson, but he said to leave them alone—"

The woman was clearly agitated, seemingly on the verge of incoherence. Parker kept his voice calm and steady as he reminded her: "Dr. Katsilometes pronounced her dead, Ms. Barnes—"

"Dr. Katsilometes wasn't there," she said, cutting him off.

It took a couple of seconds for Parker to regroup. "He signed the death certificate—"

Her voice acquired an edge. "I don't care what he signed. I'm telling you he wasn't there. Not on my shift. And not before they took June Wechsler out."

"You mean Gabriel?"

"And Bruce Wechsler."

Parker shook his head. "Let me get this straight. You're saying that June Wechsler was still alive when she was removed from Havenhurst?"

"Yes. No. I mean, I don't know. Like I said, I wasn't in the room. Mr. Gabriel said she was dead, but I couldn't tell. They had her hooked up to a portable heart-lung machine when they took her out. He said it was part of their procedure, that she had stopped breathing ten minutes before."

"You were the only person to diagnose Mrs. Wechsler's symptoms as a heart attack?"

"I talked to Dr. Katsilometes on the phone. He confirmed my diagnosis."

"But he never showed up, even knowing the gravity of the situation?" Parker asked in disbelief.

"He said he was on another emergency and couldn't make it until after midnight. He said the instructions were no heroic measures, so it wouldn't make any difference if he rushed over. He told me to give her oxygen and digitalis for the pain and he would get there as soon as he could."

"What exactly were her symptoms, Ms. Barnes?"

"Respiratory distress, severe chest pains, difficulty swallowing."

"You told all this to Jameson?"

"Yes," she said angrily. "He told me he would look into it, but in the meantime to keep quiet about it. For the good of Havenhurst, he said. He implied my job depended on my silence. But I can't keep quiet anymore. I can't stand back and let the same thing happen to Mrs. Storch—"

"Mrs. Storch?" Parker broke in, trying to catch up.

"Yes. You have to understand, Dr. Parker, my patients are my life." She paused suddenly, then her voice changed, turning falsely gay. "Uh, yes, Grace. I'll be getting off early tonight."

Parker felt like he was tuned into a radio station whose signal he kept losing. Then he heard voices in the background and understood. "Where are you? Havenhurst?"

"Uh, yes."

"You can't talk anymore?"

"That's right."

"It's very important that I speak with you," Parker said.

"I should be home around eleven-thirty. Why don't you drop by the house then?"

"I'll be there," Parker told her and hung up.

Fourteen

THE HYUNDAI WAS PARKED in Selma Barnes's driveway when Parker stepped out of his car at eleven twenty-six, but the windows of the house were dark. Parker thought that strange as he went up to the front door and rang the bell.

He could hear the bell ring inside the house, but when the echo died, no sound replaced it. He rang the bell again, with the same result, then stood back and looked again at the living room window. The lights remained off.

He stepped off the porch and went to the Hyundai and put his hand on the hood. It was warm, almost hot. Perhaps she went next door for something, Parker reasoned. But the houses on both sides were dark, too, as was most of the rest of the street, except for the blue flickerings of a television set behind an occasional front window.

Parker felt his palms and realized they were sweating. A feeling was beginning to grow in his gut, one of those sixth-sense feelings he got every once in a while, that something was terribly wrong here. The dark silence that lay against the windows suddenly seemed brooding, menacing. He went back to the door and this time knocked forcefully.

He thought he heard something behind the flimsy wood door, a muffled, whispering sound, faint and indistinct. Someone moving around inside? He pressed his ear to the door, but could not hear anything now.

He shook his head and smiled. Undoubtedly, his imagination was playing tricks on him. Cautiously, he went around the side of the house and began moving slowly down the narrow concrete walkway that ran between the house and the five-foot-high Cyclone fence that separated Selma Barnes's property from her neighbor's.

As he reached the back of the house he stopped and warily stuck his head around the corner. A wooden fence bordered the tiny backyard occupied only by an empty clothesline and a single lawn chair. Parker waited a moment, then moved slowly toward the tiny back porch. The windows at the back of the house were dark. Parker's eyes were on them when he kicked something solid. The noise it made startled him, and he stopped and looked down. Lying on its side by his right foot was a small, galvanized pail.

Parker's eyes swept the yard. A slight breeze cooled his cheek and seemed to stir the shadows thrown by the porch light from the house over the fence. His overactive imagination again. He stepped up on the back step and tried the handle of the door. It turned.

He pushed open the door and took a step into the dark room. There was just enough light to see that it was the kitchen.

"Ms. Barnes?" he called out.

No answer came back. He ran a hand along the wall beside the door, feeling for a light switch. He found one and flipped it on, flooding the room with light and allowing him a brief glimpse of the pock-marked face of the big man who stepped out from behind the door and clamped a vise-like grip onto his wrist.

Parker was yanked hard into the house and the lights went out. He struggled and flailed in the darkness, trying to wriggle free of the grip imprisoning him, but the man was incredibly strong. The man was behind him now and an arm like a thick python slithered under his right armpit and up behind his neck, bending his head forward into a half nelson. Parker stamped his foot down repeatedly as hard as he could, trying to find the bony top of the man's foot. He could smell the man's stale beer breath as his heel landed on its mark twice, and the man swore angrily and swung Parker around, hard. The arc of Parker's head was stopped by something unyielding and the room was lighted up again, this time by bright-white flames of pain, and Parker felt himself falling.

He could not tell what was up or down, but he seemed to be supported by something solid—the floor, perhaps?—then his ribs and stomach were jarred by two powerful sledge-hammer blows as a heavy foot ripped into his gut, leaving him gasping painfully for breath. He curled instinctively into a fetal position, covering his head with his hands, but no more blows came, and he became dimly and gratefully aware of the sound of footsteps pounding away from him.

He lay still for a moment, gulping in spastic lungsful of air, trying to regain control of his breathing, then rolled over onto all fours. Electric currents of pain shot through his head and body as he struggled to his feet and relocated the light switch.

He shut the back door and locked it, in case his assailant decided to return to finish the job, then turned his unfocused gaze to the room, looking for a telephone. The tiny kitchen was neat and betrayed no evidence of the intruder. Nothing seemed out of place, its Formica and stainless-steel surfaces polished and gleaming. No dirty dishes and no phone.

Parker felt a sudden wave of dizziness, then nausea, and leaned on the sink countertop for support. For a moment, he thought he was going to throw up, but then the sickness passed. He wondered if he had a concussion. He should probably have that checked out. But later.

He shook his head, trying to clear his fuzzy vision, then moved to the door across the room, feeling as if he were walking underwater. He pushed open the door and held it open, using the kitchen light to look for a lamp or a light switch in the darkened living room. He found a switch by the door and flipped it on.

Parker's vision began to clear as he scanned the small living room. It had a threadbare look, with a worn green carpet and filled with frayed, overstuffed furniture. A seventeen-inch television on rollers and a small stereo system stood against one wall, beneath a framed print of a painted calla lily. There were a couple of other cheap prints on the pale yellow walls, a set of makeshift bookshelves filled with paperback novels with worn bindings and Reader's Digest condensations. A white push-button telephone sat on the glass coffee table in front of the couch.

Parker called out Selma Barnes's name again. He

wasn't surprised when he got no answer. A narrow hallway opened off the living room and he moved down it, still a bit unsteadily. He peeked through an open bathroom door, found it empty, and continued to the end of the hall.

Two doors faced each other across the hall. One was open and he reached around to hit the light switch. It was a tiny bedroom and had a neat, unused look about it. Parker turned back to the other door.

The door was partially closed and the hinges squeaked a little as Parker pushed it open further. About halfway through its arc, the door was stopped by something, and Parker turned on the lights and looked around the edge of the door to see what it was.

The doorstop was a white nurse's shoe. The toe of the shoe was pointed straight at the ceiling and there was a foot in it. Parker stepped into the room and bent down beside Selma Barnes, who was lying on her back with her other leg bent underneath her, still dressed in her pink nurse's uniform, the skirt of which was rumpled and pulled up to just above the knees. Her face was very pale and covered with sweat. He pressed two fingers alongside her neck, feeling for a pulse, but could detect none.

He stood up and picked up the phone on the bedside table and dialed 911. He gave the dispatcher the address, requested paramedics and police, and went back to Selma Barnes.

There was no blood, her clothing was not torn, there were no gross external signs of violence on the woman's body, at least on the parts that were visible. Parker examined her throat closely, but could see no scratches or signs of bruising. He lifted her eyelids, inspecting each for petechial hemorrhaging—minute ruptures of the blood vessels in the mucous membranes that often accompany strangulation—but could not spot any.

He wished he had a magnifying glass as he looked at her hands. The nails were covered with clear polish; there were no traces of skin or blood underneath them. He examined her arms. Again, they were free of bruising or abrasions. He stood and looked the bedroom over.

This was obviously Selma Barnes's room. It was as neat as the rest of the house and as economically furnished. The twin-sized bed was neatly made and covered with a red quilted spread. There was a small maple dresser, with two matching bedside tables. He did not open the drawers, for fear of obliterating fingerprints, but there was no indication the drawers had been gone through. On the dresser was a framed color photograph of a sandy-haired man in his early twenties, standing on a beach, smiling happily. Her son? A nephew?

He turned his attention to the closet, in front of which Selma Barnes lay. The sliding mirrored door was half-open, revealing a modest wardrobe, systematically organized, dresses in one section, blouses in another, slacks in yet another.

Parker tried to get the scene down in his mind. The woman had come home, opened the front door, then come back here, most likely to change out of her uniform. Had the man been waiting behind the door, as he had with Parker, and grabbed her from behind?

The room betrayed no signs that violence had taken place here, no indications of any kind of struggle. Nothing was knocked over or broken. But that was not unusual, considering the differential in strength. The woman could have been rendered helpless in a matter of seconds.

But what would have been the motive? There were no indications of sexual assault. A burglar caught in the act, killing out of panic? There were no signs that a burglary had been in progress, no drawers pulled out, no sign that any stranger had been in the house, never mind one who had been searching for loot. Selma Barnes had come home early tonight. Had the burglar been interrupted before he could get started, first by the woman, then by Parker, and tried to sneak out the back door? But the lights had been out in the house when Parker had driven up, which meant the man would have had to have gone back through the house and turned all the lights off that Selma Barnes had turned on *before* he had any knowledge of Parker's presence. There were too many things about the scenario Parker didn't like, but right now he was in no shape to do any heavy thinking about it.

He went back over to the bureau and stared at the photograph of the boy, feeling a wave of sympathy for Selma Barnes. The photograph, the almost compulsive neatness of the place, the frayed, shabby furnishings—the woman did not have a lot to show for her forty-odd years. No wonder her patients were her life.

Parker went back out into the living room to wait for the police.

Fifteen

THEY CAME IN WAVE attacks. The paramedics and the first black-and-white arrived first, followed by more uniformed and plainclothes cops from the Garden Grove P.D., photogs, ID techs, and finally, an investigator from the coroner's office.

The two flint-faced homicide detectives who took charge of the scene were named Cabot and Armstrong, and they both knew Parker by reputation, which in all likelihood was the only thing that saved him a trip downtown.

"So the woman called you about ten," Armstrong said, looking over his notes.

"Nine fifty-one," Parker said wearily. It was after two and the fourth time he had gone over his story with various people.

"Right," Armstrong said, nodding alertly. The late hour did not seem to bother the detective. He was probably used to answering calls at times like this. Murder kept late hours. "And she said she wanted to talk to you about the Wechsler case."

Parker went through his recitation one more time.

When he was finished, Cabot asked: "You say you never saw the man who assaulted you before?"

"That's right."

"But you think you could identify him if you saw him again?"

"I'm not sure. Maybe. Things happened pretty fast."

Cabot read from his notepad: "Six two or three, two hundred and twenty pounds, brown hair, pock-marked face. That right?"

"Yeah."

Armstrong took over. "You think that the woman's phone call to you and her death are connected in some way?"

"I think the timing is pretty coincidental, don't you?"

The cop scratched his chin casually. "The world is full of coincidences, Doc. The events could be connected, but not in the way you think."

"What do you mean?"

Armstrong shrugged. "The woman was coming home early to meet you. The killer wouldn't have known that. Maybe he knew she usually didn't get home until after midnight, and picked the wrong night to burgle the house."

"There are no signs a burglary was in progress," Parker protested weakly.

"Maybe she got home before he could get started."

Parker frowned, but said nothing.

Armstrong said: "Say your theory is right, Doc, and there is a connection between the woman's call to you and her death. Say somebody found out about the call and sent someone over here to shut her up. Who'd do something like that? This Dr. Katsilo—whatever? You think doctors go around doing stuff like that?"

Cabot chimed in: "Any witnesses to the phone conversation you had with the woman?"

"No."

The detective raised an eyebrow. "Then it's just your word that she told you Katsilometes lied on Wechsler's death certificate—"

"You think I'm lying about it?" Parker asked angrily.

Cabot held up his hands in a placatory gesture. "Take it easy, Doc. No, I don't think you're lying. But just because the woman said it, that doesn't make it true. Who knows? Maybe she had a beef with the guy and was spreading stories to make him look bad."

"We'll look into it," Armstrong assured Parker.

The coroner's investigator, a tall, attractive young woman with curly blond hair, emerged from the back room. "I'm through," she said, peeling off a pair of rubber gloves.

"What's the verdict?" Cabot asked her.

"There don't seem to be any signs of external trauma. No blood, no signs of hematoma or hemorrhage. No signs of sexual assault."

Confusion clouded Armstrong's brow. "What are you saying? That she may not have been murdered?"

The woman shrugged. "I'm saying I can't see any evidence that she was, but that doesn't mean she wasn't. Cause of death will have to be determined by the autopsy."

Cabot looked at his partner and said hopefully: "Maybe she came home, found the guy in the house, and dropped dead from fright."

"We couldn't get so lucky," Armstrong said sourly.

Cabot's eyes followed the figure of the coroner's investigator as she walked out the door. "Cute."

Armstrong made a face. "Yeah, but she has to be weird being in that business."

Parker wondered what that made him. Or them. They probably never even thought about it. For cops like these, murder would always be a man's business, and that was that.

"Okay, Doc," Cabot said. "You might as well go. Any more questions, we'll be in touch."

Parker went outside. The neighborhood had come awake to view the spectacle. Curious eyes watched from front yards and windows, demonstrating that fascination with death cut across all ethnic lines. Parker would have thought they'd had enough of it where they had come from.

He caught up with the female investigator as she was getting into the county Chevy. "Miss—"

She smiled. "Wisniewski. Claire Wisniewski."

"Claire," Parker repeated. "What time does Ray usually get into the office?"

"About eight," she said, then cocked her head to one side, curiously. "I heard you mention Freeze Time in there. This have something to do with that outfit?"

"I don't know," Parker told her truthfully.

She nodded. "Those people are strange. About a year ago, I worked on one of their neuropreservation cases. It was like dealing with the members of a religious cult." She caught the question in Parker's eyes and said: "I was working for a funeral home. I'm a licensed embalmer."

"You remember the name of the case?"

She smiled. "Oddly enough, I do. Probably only because everything about the case was so damned odd. Ell-roy."

Parker took out a pen and paper and jotted it down. "You remember a first name?"

"That I don't."

"Male or female?"

"Man," she said, her eyes turning curious.

"What was the name of the funeral home you were working for?"

"Rose Mountain. What could that case have to do with this?"

"It probably doesn't. I'm just gathering all the information on Freeze Time I can."

Her eyes didn't quite believe him, but she let it go.

He asked: "How long have you been working for the county?"

"Six months."

"Like it?"

"Ray is a great guy to work for. He gives you enough credit to be able to do your job without telling you every five minutes how, you know what I mean? It's just too bad some jerks have to take advantage of that." She paused. "He worked for you in L.A., didn't he?"

"We worked together," Parker said. "I wasn't chief coroner at the time."

"He speaks very highly of you."

"I think a lot of him, too."

She shook her head. "I sure hope he doesn't get shafted. For everybody's sake."

Parker said goodnight and drove back to the hotel. Steenbargen's car was back in its space when Parker pulled into the Saddleback Inn lot. Parker parked next to it and trudged painfully up the outside stairs. A sliver of light shone between the curtains of 298 and Parker tapped lightly on the door.

"Who is it?" Steenbargen asked through the door.

"Batman," Parker answered in jest, although his mood was hardly jocular.

Steenbargen opened the door dressed in only a pair of slacks.

"You happen to have a drink in there?" Parker asked, wincing.

Steenbargen noticed the bruise blossoming along the side of Parker's face and asked: "What in the hell happened to you?"

"Let me in and I'll tell you."

Steenbargen pulled the door open and Parker hobbled in and lowered himself gently into the chair. Steenbargen unwrapped two plastic cups and poured out a couple of strong slugs of Ballantine from the bottle on the table, then sat on the edge of the bed as Parker began his chronicle of the evening's events. By the time he had finished, Parker was feeling much better, mostly due to the analgesic properties of the scotch.

Steenbargen frowned and drained his glass. "The timing does kind of stink, doesn't it?"

"The cops don't seem too bothered by it."

"What do you want me to do?"

"See if you can dig up somebody at Havenhurst who will verify Selma Barnes's story. And see what you can find out about the Storch woman. Also, the coroner's deputy at Barnes's house told me she used to work for a funeral home called Rose Mountain. About a year ago, they took in a Freeze Time case, a man named Ellroy. Maybe you can dig up the burial permit from the health department."

"Right."

Parker finished his drink, put his empty glass on the table. "Thanks for the booze." He stood up and a sharp pain in his side made him suck in a breath.

Steenbargen looked at him with concern. "You okay? Have you been to the hospital?"

Parker shook his head. "I'm all right. I'm pretty sure no damage was done that scotch and aspirin won't cure. How was Van Johnson's comeback, by the way?"

Steenbargen made a face. "Rock Hudson has about as much chance of making a comeback."

Parker smiled. "How did Marie like it?"

"She loved it." He shook his head. "If I'd known she wanted to see seventy-year-old men walk around in pajamas, I could have taken her to Havenhurst tomorrow and saved eighty bucks."

Parker said goodnight and went next door. He was exhausted, but as soon as he turned off the light and put his head on the pillow, he knew he would not be able to sleep. He was possessed by a vague restlessness; his thoughts kept coming back to the photograph on Selma Barnes's bureau.

For no good reason—there was nothing to warrant the assumption—Parker had immediately imagined that the picture had been taken many years before and that the boy was now a man. He saw the woman and the man separated by a distance greater than merely years, that picture being the only link between them.

Her patients were her life, she had said. Who, then, was that boy? Was he still alive? If he was important to her, why wasn't there more than one photo? Had she somehow lost him and if so, had it been because she had made her patients her life because she had lost him, or had she lost him because she had made her patients her life? Or had it been the other way around? Had she lost him first, and compensated by immersing herself in her work?

The picture faded and another took its place. His own son was on the bureau now.

He wanted to call Ricky, tell him he loved him. He turned into his pillow, wondering why the need should come now, so impossibly late in the night.

Sixteen

THE CORONER'S FACILITY WAS a one-story gray concrete building located behind the barbed-wire-topped gates of the Orange County jail. Parker gave the receptionist his name and was immediately ushered down a hallway to Ray Thompson's office.

The plump-cheeked, gray-bearded Thompson stood up from behind his desk and beamed as Parker entered. "God-damn, it's good to see you, Eric," he said, grasping Parker's hand warmly. "Sit, sit."

Parker took a chair and Thompson picked up the coffee mug from the desk. There was a bullet hole painted on the side and a smoking pistol, along with the legend: *Sorry I Missed You.* "You want some coffee?"

"Sounds like a winner."

"Black?"

"Cream and sugar."

Thompson nodded and left the room. He returned with a large Styrofoam cup and handed it to Parker. It was his third cup this morning, and the caffeine was just starting to kick in.

Thompson took a sip from his own mug and looked Parker over circumspectly. "You look like shit, Eric."

"Thanks. I don't look half as bad as the business I brought you last night."

Thompson raised an eyebrow. "What business is that?"

Parker told him.

When he was done, Thompson said: "You're telling me that Katsilometes falsified the death certificate?"

"That's what Selma Barnes told me."

Thompson shook his head, perplexed. "It doesn't make sense. Why would he do something like that? Technically, he wouldn't have had to be there to sign the death certificate. As long as he had seen her ten days prior to her death, he could have legally declared a cause of death on the phone."

"If Barnes had called Katsilometes and told him June Wechsler was dead, that's right, he could have. But according to what she told me, the last time he saw her, the woman was still alive. Gabriel and his people apparently barred her access to the room. When they left with her, she was hooked up to a heart-lung unit, and there was no way to tell if she was alive or dead. The only one who verified that the woman was dead was Gabriel, and he isn't legally empowered to do that."

"But why would Jameson back up Gabriel?"

Parker shrugged. "Maybe to avoid a lawsuit. Katsilometes is a contracted employee of Havenhurst, which would make the home legally a party to any screwup he made."

"And who is this Mrs. Storch?"

"One of her patients, I assume."

"You're not sure?"

"No."

"What's the deal with her?"

"My partner is trying to find that out now. Selma Barnes said she couldn't let them do the same thing to Mrs. Storch as they did to June Wechsler."

"Who is 'they'?"

"She didn't get a chance to tell me."

"And what is it 'they' did to June Wechsler?"

"I don't know," Parker said. "But an autopsy might find out. You have grounds to order one now."

"You don't know she was telling the truth," Thompson said weakly. "You have four people—Gabriel, Jameson, Katsilometes, and Bruce Wechsler—all saying one thing, and Selma Barnes saying another—"

"Selma Barnes isn't saying anything anymore," Parker said, locking stares with him across the desk.

The reminder seemed to make Thompson uncomfortable. He tugged at his beard pensively and rose. "Come on."

They went down the hall, through a door, into the receiving area. An Orange County trustee with jailhouse denims was spraying window cleaner on the glass doors, trying not to pay attention to the body bag–loaded gurney being wheeled onto the floor scale behind him. A young female deputy noted the weight and jotted it down on the clipboard in her hand. Thompson asked her: "Who is this?"

"Avila."

Thompson waved at the gurney and said to Parker: "A couple of our local fraternities of homeboys got bored spray-painting their *placa* on project walls and decided to carve it on each other's chests last night."

"What has your homicide rate been running?" Parker asked.

"About a hundred a year. Which means today is going to be a goddamned heavy day." Thompson glanced up at the two plastic entryboards on the opposite wall. One listed examination findings, the other, medical information given by the family or doctor of the deceased. "I'm taking Stan off Avila and putting him on Barnes. Where is he? I'll tell him."

"I just saw him in X-ray."

As they rounded the corner, Parker noted: "You have a lot of female deputies."

"We have four supervisors and thirteen other deputies. About half of them are women." He smiled. "We are an equal opportunity employer here."

He turned into a small room crowded with an X-ray table and dental X-ray machine. A tall black-haired man in green surgical garb had his back to them, viewing a set of dental exposures on the viewer.

"Stan," Thompson said.

The man turned around. He was very pale and had washed-out green eyes.

"Dr. Stan Merriman, Dr. Eric Parker."

Merriman pumped Parker's hand enthusiastically. "A pleasure, Doctor. I've read a lot of your articles in the *Journal of Forensic Science.* I was particularly fascinated by the piece last year you did on drug analysis of skeletonized remains. I thought it was brilliant."

"Thanks."

"Dr. Parker has a personal interest in a case that came in last night," Thompson said. "Barnes. He found the body."

Merriman's eyes widened. "Really?"

"I'd like you to do the autopsy," Thompson told him. "Max can do Avila later."

Merriman asked Parker: "Anything in particular I should look for?"

"It's wide open. I examined her superficially and could detect no obvious signs of trauma. But there was a man in her house when I got there and he was in a hell of a hurry to leave. He made his exit through me, in fact."

"Strangulation?" Merriman posited.

"It's possible, although there was no bruising on the throat where you would expect to see it, at least last night. One thing—she was diaphoretic."

"Stan is one of my best men," Thompson said. "If there is something there, he'll find it."

Merriman smiled at the compliment. "Would you like to sit in, Dr. Parker?"

Parker considered the offer, then shook his head. He did not know how much of the invitation was merely professional courtesy. Anyway, Thompson's vote of confidence in the man's abilities was good enough for him. "Thanks, but I have some things I have to do."

Merriman nodded. "I'd like to discuss that article on skeletonized remains with you sometime when you have the time. I have a similar case right now and I'd like to get your ideas."

"Anytime," Parker told him.

They went out and Thompson said: "I'm surprised you don't want to watch the autopsy."

"He doesn't need me to look over his shoulder. Anyway, I was serious about having things to do."

"One of them wouldn't be going to see Katsilometes, would it?"

Parker shrugged. "It's a nice day for a ride out to the beach. Like to tag along?" The question was almost a challenge.

Thompson shook his head. "I have things to do, too, you know—"

"Frankly, Ray, I could use your clout."

Thompson emitted an exasperated sigh. "You can be a royal pain in the ass sometimes, you know that, Eric?"

"You didn't think so when you called me up two years ago and asked me to testify at the Willie Walker hearing," Parker reminded him.

Willie Walker had been a black man who had been shot to death after being pulled over by an Orange County Sheriff for felony reckless driving. The deputy had claimed that his drawn gun that was pointed at Walker through the passenger side window had accidentally discharged when Walker, after being at a complete stop, had stepped on the accelerator, lurching the car forward. Black leaders in the community began to immediately declare the killing racist-motivated, and because of the connection between the sheriff and the Coroner's Division, Thompson had asked Parker to come in and do the autopsy. Parker's findings backed up the deputy's version of events, and in spite of numerous death threats against him, Parker had testified accordingly, clearing the Sheriff's Department of any wrongdoing.

"Remember that hearing, Ray?" Parker reminisced. "You had to keep me under twenty-four-hour protective guard for two weeks—"

Thompson tossed his hands up in surrender. "Okay, okay. I know when I'm licked. Let's go."

Seventeen

THE AUBURN-HAIRED RECEPTIONIST looked questioningly from Thompson to Parker and asked: "Do you have an appointment?"

"No."

She smiled pityingly. "Dr. Katsilometes is very busy this morning. I'm afraid you'll have to make an appointment."

Thompson looked back at the two people reading magazines on the couches in the waiting room. "He doesn't look that busy to me. Unless most of his patients are relatives of Claude Rains."

She blinked, uncomprehending. "I don't understand."

Thompson smiled tolerantly. *"The Invisible Man."*

She frowned at the joke. "No. None of his patients this morning are named Rains. Nevertheless, you'll have to make an appointment."

"I think he'll see us," Thompson said, flashing his sheriff's badge at her. "Tell him it's official business."

"Just a minute," she said, glaring at the piece of metal, and slid the frosted glass door in the partition shut. Shortly,

Katsilometes opened the door, looking slightly annoyed. The look grew more exaggerated when he spied Parker. "Come in."

They went into Katsilometes' office and sat down. The physician steepled his fingers and asked petulantly: "What's all this about official business?"

Thompson began: "You know a Selma Barnes, Dr. Katsilometes?"

Katsilometes tapped his fingers together. "Barnes, Barnes. . . . The name doesn't sound familiar. Why?"

"She was a nurse at Havenhurst. She was taking care of June Wechsler the night she died."

Recognition dawned in his eyes. "Ah, yes. I think I know who she is. What about her?"

"She died last night," Thompson said.

Katsilometes frowned. "I'm sorry to hear it. What happened?"

"We're not sure," Thompson said.

"I went over to her house to talk to her after she got off work. There was an intruder in the house. He attacked me and fled."

Katsilometes looked genuinely shocked. "You mean, she was murdered?"

"It's a distinct possibility," Parker said.

Katsilometes bit his lip anxiously. "That's terrible. But I can't understand what it has to do with me."

"A few hours before she died, she called Dr. Parker at his hotel. She said she had something very important to tell him about the Wechsler case."

Katsilometes looked away, said nothing. His hands were trembling slightly.

Thompson asked: "Where were you the night Mrs. Wechsler died, Dr. Katsilometes?"

"What kind of question is that? You know where I was—"

Thompson glanced at Parker, who said: "Selma Barnes told me that you never showed up at Havenhurst. She said from the time Gabriel and his people arrived, she was denied access to her patient, and that nobody officially verified whether Mrs. Wechsler was alive or dead—"

"Don't be ridiculous," Katsilometes interrupted. "Of course the woman was dead—"

"Then you were there?" Thompson asked.

A tic appeared at the corner of Katsilometes' mouth. "I, uh, yes, of course I was there. I signed the death certificate, didn't I?"

"We have a witness who verifies Barnes's story," Parker said.

"That's a lie," Katsilometes said, a little too forcefully. "There was nobody."

"How would you know?" Parker asked. "You weren't there."

Distress clouded Katsilometes' eyes and a slick coat of perspiration had broken out on his forehead. "I don't know what you're trying to prove with this slanderous attack on my reputation, Parker, but you won't get away with it—"

"You're denying the allegation?" Thompson cut him off.

Katsilometes' head jerked toward him. "Yes." He hesitated, then said tremulously: "You know as well as I do that as the woman's physician of record, I wouldn't have even had to show up at Havenhurst that night. The woman was under my care and she was terminal. I could have legally signed the death certificate without having been in attendance."

Thompson nodded and stood up. "And I can legally order an autopsy, which is just what I'm going to do."

The fear in Katsilometes' eyes was undeniable now. He looked like an animal that suddenly realized it had blundered into a trap.

"If you want to change your story, give me a call," Thompson said. "But if you stick to it, and I find out you've been lying, I'll have your ticket. I'll guarantee you'll never practice medicine again in this state."

The sidewalks of Laguna were filled with strollers and tourists as they drove up the Pacific Coast Highway. "You know he was lying," Parker said.

"Yeah, I know," Thompson said. "You were pushing it with that witness bit."

"He was ready to crack. I thought that might push him over the edge. Were you serious about ordering an autopsy on Wechsler?"

"We'll see," Thompson said, his tone becoming suddenly subdued.

Parker jumped on him. "What do you mean, 'we'll see'? You told me to bring you grounds. You've got them."

"If my memory doesn't fail me, I told you to bring me something compellingly strong—"

"What more do you want? You said yourself the asshole was lying through his teeth—"

"That's a gut feeling. Proving it is another thing."

"How about murder?" Parker asked hotly. "Doesn't that qualify as strong enough?"

"Whose murder are you talking about, Eric?" Thompson asked sharply. "Selma Barnes's? Even if it turns out she was murdered, there's no evidence it was tied to the Wechsler case."

Parker fell into a sullen silence.

"Anyway, Eric, aren't you breaking one of your own cardinal rules?"

Parker faced his old friend. "What's that?"

"Something you always told me," Thompson said. "Never assume anything."

Eighteen

"HEART ATTACK?" PARKER ASKED, not able to keep the surprise off his face.

Merriman nodded. "That's just a guess. There was a cessation of cardiac action, that is for sure."

"See, Eric?" Thompson chimed in. "Never assume anything."

Merriman glanced at Thompson across the chief's desk and shifted in his chair. "I looked hard for any evidence of homicide, but couldn't find any. There were no contusions, abrasions, ecchymosis. No hemorrhaging of the larynx or fractures of the hyoid bone, which would indicate strangulation. There was nothing."

"Did she exhibit any evidence of heart disease?"

"There was some arterial narrowing, but no thrombotic occlusion of any major arteries. There were no chronic valvular lesions or aortic stenosis and no apparent inflammation of the myocardium."

"Any sign of aneurysm?"

"No."

"Then what caused her heart to stop?" Parker asked.

Merriman shrugged. "That, I can't tell you. You know as well as I that a majority of sudden coronary deaths do not present fresh thrombus or myocardial infarct at autopsy. The truth is, sudden death due to coronary disease is often an enigma."

"Stress can trigger heart attack," Thompson offered. "You said yourself, Eric, that the woman was agitated when she called you. Coming home and being confronted by an intruder could have been too much for her—"

"Stress doesn't blow up a healthy heart," Parker disagreed.

"Was she exhibiting any symptoms last night?" Merriman asked.

"I'll send Wisniewski over to Havenhurst to check out that possibility," Thompson said.

Parker turned back to Merriman. "Did you find anything else? Cerebral abnormalities? Respiratory bleeding? Embolism?"

"No. Like I said, there was nothing. Of course, there's always the chance the drug screen might turn up something. The blood results should be in in a couple of days. The tissue samples should take a month or two."

Parker tossed up a hand. "I don't have a month or two. I don't even have a couple of days." He turned to Thompson. "What are you going to do, Ray?"

"About what?"

"Wechsler."

Thompson hesitated. "All we have are the unsubstantiated accusations of a woman who apparently died of natural causes—"

"With the emphasis on 'apparently,'" Parker interrupted. "There has to be something we're overlooking." He turned to Merriman, whose back had straightened at the remark and said: "I don't mean to impugn your findings, Dr. Merriman. I just can't make myself believe that the woman's death was a coincidence. The problem is, I'm operating under a deadline and it's closing in."

Merriman nodded, apparently mollified. Parker looked at Thompson and said pointedly: "How about it, Ray?"

Thompson bit his lip and stroked his beard repeatedly. Finally, he said to Merriman: "Feel up to another autopsy today?"

The pathologist shrugged. "Sure, why not?"

"I would love to assist, if the invitation is still open," Parker said.

Merriman smiled tightly. "I'd be honored, Doctor."

Nineteen

PARKER FELT LIKE A GUEST celebrity at the Grand Guignol as he walked into the autopsy room with Merriman. The word had spread and there was a noticeable pause in activity as the four pathologists and their assistants stopped cutting and weighing long enough to get a glimpse at the maestro.

On the mobile fiberglass tables before them lay their work, sliced open and sectioned, hollowed-out things that looked more like plastic anatomy dolls than human beings. The whole room, in fact, had an unreal look about it.

The average person's image of an autopsy room was a dank and bloody place, reeking of death and decay. In some primitive and antiquated facilities, that vision might have some basis in reality. But here, the stainless-steel and tiled surfaces gleamed immaculately under the bright lights, and strong suction fans above the tables effectively extracted any unpleasant odors, leaving a sanitized, state-of-the-art, surrealistic vision, nightmarish, unsettling, bizarre.

But one gets used to nightmares, and as Parker looked around the room he felt a pang of nostalgia. He had to admit, he missed it sometimes. Not performing autopsies; that was part of the job no pathologist he knew liked. How could anyone except Jack the Ripper enjoy cutting another human being into quantifiable pieces? That was the unpleasant, but necessary, part of the intellectual process, the prelude to the solving of the puzzle. One could get inured to it, but one could never quite get used to it.

No, what he missed were the resources and equipment he had had at his fingertips, the ability to experiment, test out new theories, push the limits of the science. And yes, he missed the ego-strokes that came with the power of the office. It was heady stuff, having control over that kind of a budget, moving people around. Unfortunately, that kind of control came with strings, and the strings were attached to the fingers of petty bureaucrats. Parker made a lousy dummy.

The stainless-steel door at the end of the room opened and an attendant rolled a sheet-covered table out of the refrigerated storage room to where they stood. Parker took his place in front of the scale that hung over the sink and Merriman asked: "Ready, Doctor?"

"Whenever you are."

Merriman pulled back the sheet and intoned into the overhead microphone: "The headless body is that of an undernourished, sixty-seven-year-old female. The head has apparently been surgically removed. The circumferential incision runs from the base of the neck, extending anteriorly and posteriorly, just above the clavicle. The skin has been dissected free of the connective tissue to form skin flaps, which have been stapled by skin staples over the wound."

He turned to Parker and quipped: "At least this will

be a short one. We won't have to bother with brain sections."

Merriman removed the staples, then began the external examination, going over the body carefully with a magnifying glass. After describing the sutured surgical incision, he noted no other remarkable abnormality except for the pale, blue-white color of the skin due to exsanguination, then picked up the scalpel.

Parker watched as Merriman deftly cut through the sutures, then enlarged the incision by slashing upward from shoulder to shoulder. The body gaped open, the exposed organs glistening like a basket of dark, rotten fruit.

"The organs appear to be undersized and are dark purplish-red." He asked Parker: "What do you make of that, Doctor?"

The question was not merely polite, but genuinely curious.

Parker at first had feared that Merriman might feel offended by his request to assist, especially in the light of his remarks in Thompson's office, but those fears had been quickly laid to rest by the doctor's amiable, professional manner. "They appear to be acutely congested."

"Looks almost like a drug overdose," Merriman said, drawing off a sample of blood from the heart with a syringe. He gave it to Parker, then began cutting and removing the organs. Parker recorded their weights. Considering their size, he was not surprised to find them all below normal. He was puzzled, however, when the lungs weighed in at only 600 grams each.

Merriman said: "That's only slightly above normal. I thought this woman was supposed to have died from pneumonia?"

"That's what the death certificate reads, pneumonia and heart failure." Parker sectioned both lungs and found them to be congested with fluid, but not alarmingly so. "Multiple sections show no consolidation," he said. "No evidence of respiratory bleeding."

"That would seem to rule out death by pneumonia," Merriman said. He went on to the heart.

The pericardium, the membrane covering the heart, was smooth and glistening. The myocardium was dark red, the papillary muscles not remarkable. Parker weighed the heart and found it to be 350 grams, which was normal. Dissection of the organ found no gross abnormalities. There was a ventricular thickening in the left chamber, but the valves all seemed normal. There was no evidence of thrombus or infarct, aneurysm or hemorrhage.

There was some evidence of arteriosclerosis. The left descending branch showed a narrowing of up to fifty percent at the bifurcation, the aorta showed arteriosclerotic changes, with plaques involving up to forty percent of the internal surface. "There is nothing here that would indicate that the woman died of heart disease," Parker concluded.

Merriman nodded. Both men knew that did not mean that the woman did *not* die of heart failure.

An examination of the digestive tract turned up nothing unusual. Samples of the woman's liver, heart, kidneys, pancreas, intestine, stomach, and gall bladder were taken for toxicological analysis. "I guess that's about all we can do without the head," Merriman said. "Frankly, I'm stumped on this one." He made a point of pausing. "Unless, of course, toxicology comes up with something."

"They will," Parker said. "Pentobarbital."

Merriman's black eyebrows jumped. "Pentobarbital? How do you know that?"

"It's part of the cryonics procedure," Parker said. "After the patient dies, he's put on a heart-lung machine to keep the blood oxygenated. Then they administer the drug."

"*After* death?" Merriman asked, surprised. "What in God's name for?"

"They say it quiets agonal spasms and cuts down the brain's need for oxygen."

"That's ridiculous," Merriman scoffed.

"I agree with you, but it is part of the procedure and we're going to have to take it into account."

Merriman shook his head. "I'm not sure I follow you, Dr. Parker—"

"Once this woman was hooked up to a heart-lung machine, whatever drugs were administered *even after death* would be pumped into her tissues."

"Then it will be impossible to tell if the woman was alive or dead when the drugs were administered."

"Maybe not. Any drug would be much slower to get into the spinal fluid."

Merriman's eyes narrowed. "Are you suggesting we do a spinal tap?"

Parker nodded. "Theoretically, it would take at least half an hour of perfusion to get drugs into the spine. If we find pentobarbs in the fluid, it would indicate the woman was still alive when the drug was administered."

Merriman recruited a young pathologist from the next table and together they hoisted the bony body into a sitting position. Parker selected a 16-gauge spinal needle and picked his spot low in the lumbar region. The curvature of the spine in that area had a tendency to trap fluid, and the farther away the tap was from the severed vertebrae the better, to minimize the possibility that the sample would be contaminated by the open wound.

Merriman and his helper grunted as they struggled to hold the hollowed-out, headless corpse upright. "Try to hold her steady," Parker told them as he readied the needle.

The macabre scene had the attention of even the most die-hard veterans in the room, and work came to a standstill as they watched Parker puncture the spine between L-3 and L-4. Once the needle was in, he gently slipped a catheter into it until it dipped down to the bottom of the hollow spinal column. After he had suctioned out 10 cc's of fluid, he pulled out the needle and the body was allowed to resume its reclining position on the table.

Merriman sent the fluid with the other samples they had collected to toxicology and he and Parker went out to clean up. While he was getting out of his surgical smock, Merriman said: "I must admit, I wouldn't have thought of that spinal tap business."

"I probably wouldn't have either, but I read the Freeze Time literature and was familiar with their procedures," Parker said.

"I'd still love to talk to you about your work on skeletonized remains."

Parker smiled. "Like I said, anytime."

One of the cutters came in with the message that Thompson wanted to see him in his office ASAP.

Halfway down the hallway, Parker could hear raised voices coming through Thompson's closed office door. He hesitated, knocked, and a voice shouted: "Come in."

Parker opened the door to Bruce Wechsler pacing furiously in front of Thompson, who was seated at his desk. He whirled around to face Parker. His face looked like a bag full of blood that was about to burst. "You. You're the cause of this."

The man looked ready for a seizure. His entire body was trembling violently. "Take it easy, Mr. Wechsler," Parker began.

"Don't tell me to take it easy! What right do you have to butcher my mother against my wishes?"

"We don't butcher people," Parker replied, attempting to keep his voice calm. "As far as the right, Ray Thompson has the legal right to order an autopsy on any person whose death he deems to be equivocal."

Wechsler took a step toward him. There was a white froth of spittle on his lips. "*Equivocal?* There was nothing equivocal about my mother's death. A doctor was present—"

"That does seem to be the question, doesn't it?" Parker said, smiling.

The smile seemed to infuriate Wechsler even more. His eyes narrowed and his hands balled into fists. "You're calling me a liar?"

"I'm not calling anybody a liar," Parker replied. "I do find it curious that you haven't even asked me what the autopsy on your mother found."

"I don't have to," he sneered. "I *know* what you found. Nothing."

"That's right," Parker said. "Nothing. Which means that your mother didn't die of pneumonia, as it says on the death certificate."

Wechsler eyed him hotly. "Just what are you trying to imply, Parker?"

"Me? Nothing. Yet."

Wechsler pointed an accusatory finger. "I know all about you, Parker. Everybody knows you're nothing but a publicity-crazy opportunist. That's why the county cut you loose. You're only involved in this for what you can get out of it. Well, your meddling is going to backfire on you this time. I'll have your ass for what you've done. Yours and Thompson's, too. I'll sue you for every cent you have."

He slammed out of the office and Parker said: "Katsilometes didn't waste much time spreading the word."

"I think he's serious about suing."

Parker took the chair in front of the desk. "On what grounds? That you did your duty as coroner?"

"I'm not saying he can win. But the publicity is something I'd just as soon avoid at the moment."

"I don't think he's going to want it, either."

"So you found no pneumonia?"

"Some, but she didn't die of it, I'll stake my reputation on that."

"You might have to. What about heart failure?"

Parker shrugged. "There were no gross abnormalities of the woman's heart, nothing that would indicate that she died of heart disease. But it's like Merriman said earlier, sudden cardiac death is still pretty much a mystery."

Thompson made a face. "In other words, there's no way to say she did or didn't die of heart failure?"

"Maybe, maybe not. That could depend on what your toxicology lab comes up with on the tissue and fluid samples we sent over."

"I'll call the lab and see if I can get a rush on the blood. If they can run it right away, they should have results within a couple of hours."

"I have to go back to L.A. tonight, but I'll be around the hotel until about six or so."

"I'll call you as soon as I hear something," Thompson promised.

Twenty

STEENBARGEN WAS NOT BACK when Parker got back to the hotel, so he ate a sandwich alone in the coffee shop. He was paying his check when he was paged to the phone. He took the call in the lobby.

"The tox results just came in," Ray Thompson said.

"And?"

"It will be at least a month before we get the tissue analysis back, but pentobarbital in significant amounts showed up in the blood and spinal fluid."

"Then she was alive when the drug was administered," Parker said excitedly.

"Not necessarily."

"What do you mean?"

"Merriman says that if she had been hooked up to the heart-lung machine for longer than half an hour, the drug would have been pumped into her spine, even if she was dead. He also seems to think that there's a serious question whether the spinal fluid was contaminated after the woman was decapitated. He thinks we would have to have the woman's head to determine for sure whether she was alive when the drug was given to her."

"He didn't voice that opinion during the autopsy," Parker said, feeling somewhat betrayed. Not because the man had a professional difference of opinion. In an area as nebulous and theoretical as this, that was natural. But that he had waited until now to express it. Perhaps Parker had misjudged the man and he did harbor some professional jealousy.

"Nevertheless, he is expressing it now."

"Wechsler and Gabriel would certainly fight that move."

"And I'm not sure we could win," Thompson said. "There was a similar case a few years ago in Riverside. The coroner tried to obtain a woman's head from a cryonics firm there on the grounds that her death was suspicious. The cryonics people refused to give it up, saying that the entire suspension procedure would be irrevocably ruined by an autopsy, and the courts backed them up."

"So what are you going to do?"

"I have an appointment with the district attorney in the morning. I'll explain the situation to him and see what course of action he wants to take."

"What are you going to do about the official cause of death?"

"I'm going to leave that open for the time being."

"Bruce Wechsler isn't going to like that."

"I don't give a shit what he likes," Thompson said testily.

"If the D.A. decides to go after the head, Wechsler will sue for sure."

"That'll be the D.A.'s decision. It'll be out of my hands."

Parker was beginning to see the pattern of Thompson's strategy.

He went up to his room and called Leah Wechsler. She sounded stunned by the news of the autopsy. "You're saying mother was *murdered*?"

"I'm saying the pentobarbital might have been a contributing factor to her death. The big question is whether she was alive when they gave it to her."

"What is your opinion? Was she?"

"It think it's possible, if not likely."

She jumped on the statement. "If the coroner rules mother's death a homicide, and Bruce and Gabriel were participants, neither of them can benefit from her death."

"I'm afraid Ray Thompson isn't willing to go that far out on a limb at this time."

Her voice turned angry. "What do you mean? You just said in your opinion, the drugs contributed to her death—"

"I said it was possible," Parker corrected her. "The pathologist who did the autopsy, Dr. Merriman, is taking the position that it would be necessary to autopsy your mother's head before any determination of homicide could be made."

"Her head?" she repeated, as if not quite comprehending.

"When brain death occurs," Parker explained, "the brain immediately begins to swell, and circulation is cut off. Even being hooked up to a heart-lung machine—which is part of the Freeze Time process—the flow of blood in the brain would be drastically reduced."

She blinked in confusion. "So?"

"So, according to Gabriel, your mother was dead before he went to work on her. Allegedly, they administered pentobarbital as part of their procedure postmortem." Parker paused significantly. "But if she wasn't dead—if she was still alive when the drugs were administered—one would expect to find significant amounts of pentobarbital in the brain tissue."

"Then let's get her head," she said firmly.

"It's not that easy. Your brother and Gabriel would undoubtedly fight any effort in that direction. They would undoubtedly argue that an autopsy of the head would result in a destruction of the suspension process. Unfortunately, they have legal precedent on their side."

"In other words," she said, her voice turning angry, "$5,000 and an autopsy later, I'm back to where I started—nowhere."

"You're not back to where you started," he said, trying to calm her down. "We've established that there is reason at least to question further that the circumstances of your mother's death were suspicious. We know definitely that she was given pentobarbital—"

The woman would not be placated. "I could have read that in one of Gabriel's pamphlets. I didn't need to hire you."

She was beginning to seriously irritate him. "You're right, Ms. Wechsler, you didn't. The balance of your retainer will be mailed to you as soon as I get back to L.A."

"You don't intend to quit?" she asked, surprised.

"You are obviously unhappy with our work."

"Don't be so goddamned touchy," she snapped. "So what do we do?"

Parker shook his head. He was just a simple man, not able to keep up with the woman's mercurial mood swings. "My advice would be wait and see what the district attorney intends to do. If he decides to push it, your problem is solved, at the county's expense. If not, you can always petition the court in a civil action. I can prepare an affidavit, laying out the reasons why I think the head should be acquired for autopsy."

"That sounds like a reasonable approach," she said, her voice calm once again.

He told her he would call her tomorrow and hung up, wondering if insanity was a genetic trait in the Wechsler family.

He was packing his bag on the bed when he was interrupted by a knock on the door. He opened it and Steenbargen strolled in casually. The investigator eyed the open bag and said: "Getting ready to leave?"

Parker nodded. "The autopsy on June Wechsler has been done."

Steenbargen sat in a chair and listened cross-legged while Parker filled him in on the day's events. When he had finished, Steenbargen asked: "Think Wechsler's threats have made Ray a little gun-shy, and he's trying to pass the buck to the D.A.?"

"That's the way it looks."

"It could end up backfiring on him. If the D.A. decides to go after the head, Wechsler will sue for sure. And the possibility of damages in a case like that would be astronomical."

Parker nodded tiredly, rubbed his eyes. "I don't think anybody is going to make any concerted effort to go after the head. Even if they succeeded in getting it, there would still be a margin of uncertainty, albeit a slight one, that June Wechsler was still alive when they shot her full of drugs. I don't think they'll risk the chance of embroiling the county in a big legal battle knowing that."

"So the death stays undetermined?"

Parker shrugged helplessly.

"What about Selma Barnes?"

Parker frowned. "Officially, it's a heart attack."

"Heart attack?"

"That was my reaction, too."

"Did she have a history of heart problems?"

"Not that anybody knows about. And the pathologist could find no evidence of coronary disease."

"Then how the hell does he figure heart attack?"

"He couldn't find anything else. There were no signs of trauma and her drug screen was clean."

"Think he missed something?"

"I have no reason to think so. According to Ray, he's one of his best men. What did you find out at Havenhurst?"

"Barnes's supervisor—Sylvia Gradishar—told me Barnes went home early last night on instruction from Jameson."

"Jameson?"

Steenbargen nodded. "Apparently, he issued a memo last week instructing them to cut back the hours of employees who had accumulated too much overtime. Barnes had piled up some extra hours over the past couple of weeks, so Gradishar sent her home."

"She wasn't complaining of not feeling well? No chest pains, dizziness, nausea?"

"Gradishar didn't mention it, and I'm sure she would have."

"Did you talk to anybody who was working the night Wechsler died?"

"Two other nurses. Both claim they were busy elsewhere that night. There were apparently a couple of other emergencies and they were short-staffed because two girls called in sick. Neither of them saw Katsilometes, but that doesn't mean he wasn't there."

"You believe them?"

"Frankly, I do."

"Where was this Gradishar that night?"

"Off. Barnes apparently filled in as head nurse on those nights."

"Did Barnes tell any of her coworkers the same story she told me?"

"Not that I talked to. My asking them about it was the first they'd heard of it."

"What about Jameson?"

"He denies the whole thing. Says he can't imagine why the woman would have made up such a story, except that she had put in a lot of extra hours lately and had been suffering from work-related stress. He says she always did get too emotionally involved with her patients and took it very personally when one of them died. He says he noticed that Barnes was all keyed-up after Wechsler died, which was one reason he wanted her hours cut back. Gradishar confirmed that Barnes had seemed on edge lately."

"What about Storch?" Parker asked.

"She's a patient there, all right."

"You talked to her?"

"Yeah. She's eighty-one and pretty feeble. She's still alert, though. She's been there about six months. No living relatives."

"What about cryonic suspension?"

"I asked her about it. She had no idea what I was talking about."

"Another dead end," Parker said.

"Maybe not," Steenbargen said, stroking his mustache. "Your Ellroy lead panned out. First name, Lawrence. Died 5-7-88. Cause of death, cerebral hemorrhage. Guess who signed the death certificate?"

Parker gave him the answer he had been cued-up for. "Katsilometes."

"Right on," Steenbargen said with a sly grin. "Not only that. Mr. Ellroy died at Havenhurst, where he had been a resident for a year prior to his death."

Parker pondered the significance of that. "Two cryonic suspensions from Havenhurst within a year, both taken care of by Katsilometes? That would seem to be highly unlikely."

Steenbargen shook his head and continued to stroke his mustache. "Three."

Parker looked at him, hard. "Huh?"

"Three. I should say, three that I could document. The third was a Mrs. Beryl Mapes, who died at Havenhurst on 6-8-88 of heart failure. Again, Katsilometes signed the death certificate."

Parker listened in thoughtful silence while Steenbargen went on. "After finding out about Mr. Ellroy, I was naturally curious as to exactly how many bodies were stored at Freeze Time and where they'd come from. The problem is, none of the cases are cross-referenced according to method of disposal. You have to have the deceased's name in order to check out the burial permit. Fortunately, my experience working for a county bureaucracy taught me that there is always one person in any government office who knows everything that goes on in that office."

"And you found him."

"Her," Steenbargen corrected him. "Grace Lagitutta. Grace is the head clerk. She oversees the filing of all the burial permit applications for the county. She also has a memory like an elephant. She remembered the Mapes case."

"Maybe Chaney wasn't so crazy after all with his 'angels of death.' "

"My thought exactly."

The wheels were turning rapidly in Parker's mind. "I'd be very interested to know who owns Havenhurst."

"I'm way ahead of you," Steenbargen said. "A California corporation. C.E.D., Inc."

"Who are the officers?"

"Jameson, president. And guess who is vice president and a principal stockholder? None other than your friend and mine, William Barnaby."

"A minor fact he neglected to mention during the meeting." Parker considered. What reason would Barnaby have for concealing his interest? And what else had he neglected to mention?

"Should I give it another day?" Steenbargen asked.

Parker nodded. They had come this far. It wouldn't hurt to turn over a few more rocks.

Twenty-one

RUSH-HOUR TRAFFIC AND a three-car pileup on the freeway stretched the fifty-minute drive from Santa Ana into two and a half hours, and Parker pulled into his driveway at nine-twenty, wrung-out and exhausted.

As he reached the door, he could hear the phone ringing inside. He swore, fumbling with his keys on the dark doorstep, knowing that the principal scenario of his life was going to be replayed. He would get the door open, reach the phone, and it would stop ringing. But the ringing continued. He finally managed to get the right key inserted in the lock and pushed open the door. He took two steps inside the house and was reaching for the light switch, when a heavy arm coiled around his throat, effectively shutting off his oxygen supply and any impulse he might have had to yell.

He instinctively thrashed, grabbed the beefy arm and tried to loosen its grip. He realized immediately that would be useless against the police chokehold. The man wasn't trying to strangle him, just put him out, and Parker knew that wouldn't take long, perhaps five seconds, before the lack of blood to his brain due to the pressure on his carotids would do just that. He fought down the panic and tried to remember the moves he had learned during his training at the police academy.

He bent his knees and turned his hips to the right, pivoting on his right foot. From a semisitting position, he turned his body to the left. The attacker's superior weight and strength were now being used against him and Parker swung the man over his hip. The man swore, surprised, and his grip loosened as he fell backwards with Parker on top of him. Parker put a hand out to brace his fall and felt his finger go into something soft. An eye.

Parker was deafened by a bellow of pain. He pushed off the man, trying desperately to get away, but a hand seized the lapel of his jacket and held him down. Parker struck out repeatedly with his fists and several times they found a face—but the grip on his coat didn't loosen.

Parker squirmed and wriggled and bucked and finally managed to get a shoulder out of the jacket. He tore his arm out and shed the garment like a dead skin, then scuttled away on all fours into the darkness. His escape seemed to infuriate the intruder, who growled in a voice like sandpaper: "I'll kill you, you motherfucker. When I get my hands on you, I'll break you into fucking pieces."

Parker felt like a roach as he skittered to the wall and crouched behind his big easy chair. His hand struck the brass base of the standing lamp. He felt around the base for the cord and yanked it from its socket, seeking refuge in the dark. The light was his enemy now. As long as it remained dark, Parker had an advantage. At least he knew the layout of the room. He wished he'd stuck his fingers in both the man's eyes.

The assailant stood up and moved slowly toward the chair. Parker could make out the dark, slouching shape against the sliding glass door that led out to the patio. Desperately, he looked around the familiar space, his eyes trying to probe the darkness, trying to visualize the room, what he could use for a weapon.

The man would be on him in a few seconds. Parker knew he had to do something quick, but the minute he moved away from the chair, the man would be sure to hear him. The cold metal of the lamp gave him an idea. Grasping the base with his right hand and the pole with his left, he stood up suddenly. Tilting it forward like a lance, he emitted a high-pitched war cry and charged.

The torch caught the stunned intruder in the chest and sent him hurling backwards, crashing through the sliding glass door. His back hit the porch railing, splintering the wood, and he screamed as he flew off into nothingness, his arms and legs flailing uselessly as he disappeared from sight.

Breathing hard, Parker dropped the lamp and carefully opened the shattered door. There was blood on the jagged pieces of glass that were still in the frame, a trail of blood droplets and glass fragments on the wood slats of the patio. Parker crunched over to the edge and looked down.

The man was lying twenty feet below, his upper body enshrouded in a clump of sagebrush. He did not appear to be moving. Parker went back inside and turned on the lights, grabbed a flashlight from the kitchen cupboard and started out. At the front door, he paused, then went back and picked up the brass poker from the fireplace set. No sense taking any chances.

He went out the front door and around the side of the

house, making his way slowly, carefully down the steep slope to where the man lay. The man still had not moved and when Parker parted the bush, he saw why.

The man's head was jammed up against a large, blood-soaked rock, at an angle that would have been impossible to attain with an unbroken neck. Purely as a formality, he picked up one of the rag-doll arms and felt the wrist for a pulse. Nothing.

Parker stared at the bloody, pock-marked face. He had no doubts that it was the same man who had attacked him at Selma Barnes's. He turned away, feeling slightly nauseous.

Parker's legs were rubbery by the time he got back up to the house, but little of it had to do with the climb. He had just come very close to being murdered. Instead, he himself had killed. Not murder. Self-defense. There was more than a slight difference. He stopped on his doorstep and looked at his hands. They were trembling violently.

He opened the front door and was on his way to the phone, when his foot kicked something, sending it rebounding noisily off the baseboard of the wall. His eyes searched for the object, spied it against the carpet, ten feet away. Curious, he went over and picked it up.

It was a small prescription vial with a rubber top, the kind used for giving injections. He read the label. Magnesium sulfate, fifty percent solution. Sonofabitch.

Whatever questions that might have remained about the intruder's intent were effectively answered by the bottle in his hand. It also told him what had happened to Selma Barnes.

Twenty-two

THE LIVING ROOM WAS a hive of activity as the team of evidence men went about their business, gathering fibers and glass slivers, dusting for fingerprints and checking doors and windows for signs of forced entry. Parker watched the ID tech seated at his dining room table carefully lift a latent print from the prescription bottle he had found. "Magnesium sulfate. What the hell is it?" said a voice beside him.

Parker turned to face Steve Morgino. The L.A.P.D. homicide detective had aged at least ten years in the four Parker had known him. His sandy hair was rapidly receding, his eyes were heavily bagged, and his once athletic frame was now paunchy. Parker had gotten to know Morgino casually while he had been chief coroner and had found him to be intelligent and observant, with an intensely serious, almost evangelical approach to his work. Which was perhaps why he looked at least five years older than the thirty-five he was.

Humor—however black—was a survival trait in police work, and those without it were marked for early burnout.

Parker could already see the telltale signs in Morgino's face, the armored, almost hostile look in the eyes, the tightness around the mouth, the tense, clipped speech, the little displays of defensive body posture. He seemed to be taking this more personally than Parker.

"A CNS depressant."

"A what?"

"Central nervous system depressant. It's commonly used in cases of acute nephritis or in obstetric patients who have toxemic pregnancies, to prevent seizures. It slows down the action of the central nervous system."

"And it'd kill you?"

"Ten cc's of it would, if it was administered intravenously. Normal doses of mag sulfate are handled rapidly by the kidneys, but not that kind of concentration. The blood pressure would plummet, causing the heart to stop. It would look like a heart attack."

Morgino nodded. "It fits. We found a busted syringe in his pocket."

"He must have figured to render me unconscious with the chokehold, then inject the drug in a vein. He must have used the same MO with Selma Barnes."

"Why wasn't it picked up at the autopsy?"

"They wouldn't normally run a toxicology check for magnesium."

"Why not?"

"It's an element normally found in the body, so it would be hard proving an overdose. Also, it's not a drug commonly used to kill people."

"Well, it sure as hell was in this case," Morgino said. "You trying to tell me there's no way to prove the woman was murdered?"

"There might be, if they can find a needle mark. The pathologist didn't spot one, but that doesn't mean it's not there. If the needle is skinny enough, those things can be a bitch to see."

Morgino sighed in frustration. "So where in the hell would the guy have gotten the stuff? And how would he know how to use it?"

"Both good questions. You find any ID on him?"

"Driver's license, that's about all. Name was Donald Aiken. Ring a bell?"

"No. You know where he was working?"

"Not yet, but I will."

"The woman was a nurse. Maybe this Aiken worked with her. The convalescent home would have drugs. Maybe he worked at a hospital."

"A male nurse?" Morgino postulated.

Parker shrugged. His mind was not working too well.

Morgino rattled on: "It would have been a hell of a lot harder proving murder if he had eliminated you. You were the only one who could identify him."

"Actually, I'm not sure I could have."

"But he didn't know that. He must have thought about it and decided not to take the chance."

"His motive for killing me is logical. The big question is, why did he eliminate Selma Barnes?"

"That's *our* job," Morgino said with what sounded like an undertone of warning in his voice.

"Don't worry, I don't intend to do it for you," Parker assured him.

Morgino nodded, but he didn't look as if he quite believed that.

The ID tech finished his job on the bottle, then put

everything away in his evidence case. "That should about do it."

Parker glanced around at the shattered door, the glass-littered carpet, the fingerprint powder that seemed to cover everything. "For you, maybe."

The evidence man shrugged and went out, passing Herb Cravey, who came in through the front door. Cravey was a tall, rangy, hawk-faced investigator who had been one of Steenbargen's hand-picked team at the coroner's office for over six years. Parker and he had never had much to say to each other, aside from the usual hellos and how are yous, but the man had always been quietly competent, a quality Parker valued.

"You sure did a number on that clown, Chief," the investigator remarked casually. "If the broken neck didn't kill him, the skull fracture did."

"Better not let Jim Phillips hear you calling me Chief."

Cravey scratched his head. "Why not? I call him Chief, too. Besides, if he can't take a joke, fuck him."

Parker smiled. "How are things at the office?"

Cravey shrugged noncommittally. "Okay."

It was a bitter pill for Parker to swallow, but the department was better off without him, which was why he had resigned. His personally picked replacement, Jim Phillips, aside from being a top-notch forensic pathologist and competent administrator, kept just the kind of low profile the County Board of Supervisors wanted after Parker's stormy, flamboyant term as chief coroner. Phillips abhorred the public spotlight, kept the proverbial skeletons in their various closets, and always cleared his statements to the media with the board. Because of that, budget allocations were promptly released, requests for additional staff and equipment were approved, the bodies rolled in, the bodies rolled out. The logjams that had plagued the later Parker years, a result of the efforts of a few powerful political enemies to make him look bad, were conspicuously absent.

Parker liked to think that his fall from grace had been because of his unwavering principles, his stubborn unwillingness to compromise the truth. But he often wondered if his motives had been all that noble. Perhaps it had been rooted in something more petty in his character and he had merely fallen through pride. At those times, he looked back and thought perhaps he should have just shut up and done what he was told. But that would have been like telling a dog not to bark at a strange sound; it was not in his nature. If that was a character flaw, he knew he would die with it.

"Did you know the dead guy, Chief?" Cravey asked.

"I met him once, briefly."

"You two just didn't hit it off, or was it something more personal?"

"He was at the scene of a possible murder. I was a witness."

"He did the murder?"

"That's my guess. I can't think of another reason for him to have been waiting for me inside my house with a syringe loaded with magnesium sulfate."

Cravey raised an eyebrow. "Magnesium sulfate? That's a new one on me."

The phone rang and Parker answered it. "Eric, this is Jim Gordon."

"Yeah, Jim?" he said listlessly.

"I tried to reach you earlier, but you weren't home—"

"That was you?" Parker asked.

"Yeah," the prosecutor replied, puzzled by the question. "Did you get a chance to go over that material I gave you?"

"I read it."

"And?"

"I can see what you mean about the first case."

"You're still going to testify for the defense?"

"Yes."

"You're going to help cut this fucking monster loose?" Gordon asked in disbelief.

The conversation was beginning to grate on Parker. He had monsters of his own to deal with right now. "I'm going to answer the questions that are put to me. That's all I can do."

"You know as well as I do that there are pertinent questions I can't ask—"

"That's your problem," Parker snapped.

"It's society's problem if this creep skates."

"There is nothing I can do about that," Parker said angrily. "I can only describe what I found and offer the best interpretation of those findings. I can't rectify the mistakes the system made. It isn't my goddamn job to win your case for you or Ennis's for him."

"But your opinion is?"

"Ask me that in court," Parker said and slammed down the receiver.

He slumped back in his chair and massaged his temples with his fingertips. He felt a twinge of guilt about jumping on Gordon. He had overreacted, but he was not in the mood to deal with courtroom strategies at the moment. He felt totally drained, wrung-out, and he wanted these people out of his house. He needed solitude, a stiff drink, and eight hours of sleep, preferably in that order. He was immensely relieved when Morgino put away his notebook and said: "I'll get out of your hair, Dr. Parker. Probably be in touch with you tomorrow."

"I'll be at the office."

Morgino went out and Cravey said: "I'll be on my way, too."

Parker nodded tiredly. "Tell everybody hello for me."

The front door closed, mercifully leaving Parker alone with his thoughts. He dreaded going through the story again, but knew he had to. After shocking Steenbargen out of a sound sleep with the facts and spending a full minute assuring him he was indeed all right, he phoned the Orange County Coroner's Office. After 5:00 P.M., the telephone rang directly into the investigator's room, and he identified himself and asked for Wisniewski. There was a brief wait and she came on the line.

"Hello, Dr. Parker. What can I do for you?"

"Has Selma Barnes's body been released for burial yet?"

"Just a sec and I'll check the board." She was off the line for a moment, then returned. "Tomorrow morning."

"Merriman or somebody is going to have to go over the body again and look for a needle mark," Parker told her. "The man who attacked me in her house just paid me a visit. He had a hypo full of magnesium sulfate. I think that's how Barnes was killed. The diaphoresis, all the other physical symptoms fit."

"Magnesium sulfate?" she asked, intrigued. "I've never come across an overdose of that."

"Tell the toxicology people to run her blood, tissues, and vitreous humor for magnesium concentrations. If the levels are high enough, it would go a long way to make a case for murder."

"Got it." She hesitated and her voice grew concerned. "Are you okay?"

"I'm fine."

"Did they catch the guy?"

"He's dead."

"Who is he?"

"His name is Aiken," Parker said tiredly. "They don't know any more about him than that right now."

He gave her Morgino's name and told her he would be in his office if anyone had any questions. The telephone receiver felt as if it weighed ten pounds as he hung it up.

He went into the kitchen and poured himself a double vodka and carried it back into the living room. A chilly breeze blew in through the empty door frame, stirring the loose papers and pages of journals scattered around the room. He stood in front of the gaping hole, staring out at the night.

The scene kept replaying in his mind, the shape (Aiken, he had a name now) smashing through the door, the sound of the breaking glass, the scream of pain changing to terror as he plummeted to his death. Parker had worked on thousands of men who had been the victims of violence, but he had never before been the one who had wrought that violence. He had now struck up a new acquaintance with death, a somehow more personal one.

He could sort out exactly how he felt about it tomorrow, he thought as he carried the drink into the bedroom. Right now, all he could think about was sleep.

Twenty-three

PARKER GLANCED APPREHENSIVELY IN the rearview mirror, wondering if it was just his imagination, or was he really being followed? He was sure he had seen the same white Dodge Lancer behind him twice now since he had started out from home—or certainly it *looked* like the same car.

His imagination, he decided. After last night, anybody's nerves would be on edge. Then he thought about the last time he had thought his imagination had been playing tricks on him, and his hands began to sweat. He could not let this thing make him paranoid. How did the saying go? Just because you're paranoid, it doesn't mean they're *not* out to get you.

Parker kept his eyes glued to the mirror and the car turned off, disappearing down a side street. He let out a breath, feeling a wave of relief. He shook his head at his silliness and found himself whistling, something he seldom did, on the rest of the drive to the small neighborhood park where he was to meet Brian Westberg.

Westberg was already there, waiting at the baseball diamond with Gary Biderhoff, a Deputy D.A. for the County of Los Angeles. They watched Parker approach, and even at a distance, the two men, both dressed in conservative business suits, gave the impression of great seriousness.

Violence on their minds, Parker mused. Like him, they made their livings from violence. Other people's violence, but violence nonetheless. Westberg, short, middle-aged and balding, was a successful criminal attorney who had never defended a guilty client (or at least one who admitted it), and charged top dollar to convince juries of that fact. Biderhoff, a handsome, athletically built blond giant, looked more like a linebacker than an attorney, which was just fine with him. His appearance had worked to his advantage more than once in a trial, by lulling the opposition into a false sense of superiority and setting them up for a blindside sack.

Westberg hailed Parker heartily. "Good morning, Eric! Ready to convince this gentleman he hasn't got a case?"

"I'm going to try," Parker said, shaking hands with both of them.

"Good luck," Biderhoff scoffed. "I know why we're out here, Westberg. It's called 'Let's Make a Deal.' But I told you, there aren't going to be any deals on this one. Your client is going up for the max."

"We'll see," Westberg said cryptically.

Parker led them behind the wire batter's cage to the wooden picnic table. There, two weeks before, Evelyn Carlucci had been discovered, battered and unconscious, apparently the victim of a vicious beating.

Mrs. Carlucci regained consciousness in Mercy Hospital Emergency and identified her husband, who had been arrested numerous times before for spousal abuse and assault, as her assailant. Police went immediately to the Carlucci home, one block away from the baseball diamond, where they found the two Carlucci children, ages four and five, home alone. Neighbors told the patrolmen that there had been a violent domestic argument at the Carluccis' earlier, apparently not an uncommon occurrence.

Philip Carlucci was located an hour later in a nearby bar, drunk and belligerent. After a scuffle with the police, he was taken to the nearby police station and booked for felonious assault and felony child endangerment. Carlucci acknowledged that he and his wife had argued earlier, but denied having beaten her, claiming he had stormed out of the house soon after the argument had started, telling her he was moving out.

The case seemed to be open and shut. The prosecution had motive, opportunity, and an eyewitness to the crime—the victim herself. In fact, the only mystery to Biderhoff was what Westberg could hope to accomplish by bringing in a heavy hitter like Eric Parker. He had no doubts about the verdict if the case went to trial, as it inevitably would. Still, Parker's presence made Biderhoff uneasy. The man had a reputation for coming up with the unexpected. That was silly. What could he possibly come up with? He would soon find out as Parker walked over to the batter's cage and pointed up at the wire mesh.

"We found blood on the wire up to three meters, spaced a little over a meter apart, in a diagonal zigzag pattern," Parker said. "The blood type was O, the same as Mrs. Carlucci's. The spacing of the stains is consistent with her reach, if she had been trying to climb the fence. As you know, the palms of her hands were abraded when she was admitted to the hospital. We also found bloodstains on the picnic table. Same blood type—O."

Parker was leading up to something and Biderhoff had a feeling he was not going to like whatever it was. "What exactly are you trying to say, Doctor?"

Parker looked at the man steadily. "I'm saying that in my opinion, Mrs. Carlucci's injuries were self-inflicted."

The prosecutor's mouth dropped open in disbelief. "*Self-inflicted?* You can't be serious."

"Oh, but I am."

Biderhoff shook his head in bewilderment. "Let me get this straight. You're saying the woman wandered out here and beat herself up until she lost consciousness? Then made up a cock-and-bull story that her husband did it?"

"You have to admit," Westberg broke in, "the woman has an axe to grind."

"Sure," Biderhoff scoffed. "I'd have an axe to grind, too, if my husband had kicked the shit out of me half a dozen times over the past four years. The man is a goddamned menace. He should be put in a cage."

"Maybe he should, but not for this," Parker said.

"Okay," Biderhoff said, waving his arms. "You tell me how the woman beat herself senseless—"

Parker smiled indulgently. "I didn't say she did. I just said her injuries were *self-inflicted.*"

Biderhoff said: "I'm afraid you've lost me, Dr. Parker."

"At Mercy Emergency, Mrs. Carlucci was awake, but incoherent. Her speech was slurred and her pupils were widely dilated, which would fit the diagnosis of concussion. But that diagnosis was based on Mrs. Carlucci's appearance. The doctors *assumed* she had been beaten. But her symptoms would have also fit something they didn't check for—a drug overdose."

Biderhoff was clearly becoming agitated. "Drug overdose? There's no evidence that Mrs. Carlucci had taken drugs—"

Parker held up a finger. "Ah, but there is." He took a step away and swung around to face the prosecutor. "When Mr. Carlucci made bail the next day and went home, he was understandably in a nervous state, so he went to his medicine cabinet to get a Valium, which had been prescribed by his doctor. To his surprise, he found the empty prescription bottle in the trash. He knew that the bottle had contained at least eight tablets, as he had taken one of the pills the day before. He concluded his wife must have taken the pills. He was right. Mrs. Carlucci, upset by her husband's claim that he was leaving her, swallowed the pills, then wandered in a daze out of the house."

"That's your evidence?" Biderhoff scoffed. "Carlucci's word?"

"When she was admitted to Mercy, a blood sample was taken for typing, just in case she had internal injuries and had to be transfused. Luckily, they still had the sample when I checked. I had a chemical analysis done of the sample. The woman had ingested a good quantity of Valium."

"Even if she took the Valium, it doesn't mean Carlucci didn't beat her up," Biderhoff protested. "What about all the cuts and bruises on her face and body?"

Parker said calmly, "When I examined the photographs of Mrs. Carlucci's injuries, there was something about them that bothered me, something that wasn't quite right. The backs of her hands were badly abraded, as were the left side of her face, her knees, the tops of her feet. She also had large, multiple contusions on the point of her left hip. The pattern of the injuries baffled me. Then I talked to the emergency room nurses who were working when Mrs. Carlucci was brought in. They said she was babbling the same thing, over and over, about having to get back to her children. She kept saying that she had climbed up a big wall and swum across a big lake in an effort to get back to them. Suddenly, the pattern of her injuries made sense. She'd gotten them swimming."

Biderhoff smiled sardonically. "I'm glad that makes sense to you, Doctor, because it doesn't to me."

"There's the wall," Parker said forcefully, pointing at the batter's cage. He then turned and pointed at the picnic table. "And *there* is her lake."

Biderhoff looked from one to the other, then glanced at Westberg, who said, "Go on, Eric."

"When the Valium took effect, Mrs. Carlucci didn't know what she was doing. She wandered out of the house and over here to the park, where she blacked out. In that semidream state, she suddenly remembered that she had left her children, and her maternal instincts took over. She knew she had to get back to them, but there were obstacles in her way—the wall and the lake. She cut her hands trying to scale the wall, then she began to swim on the picnic table. If you will examine the pattern of her injuries—her left hip, the left side of her face—you'll see that it is consistent with someone doing the freestyle, turning her face and hip into the hard wood surface."

Biderhoff looked dumbfounded, but said nothing.

"I asked you here so that you'd know what I'm going to present as a defense," Westberg said. "If you want to push ahead with a trial, I thought I'd give you the opportunity to hear what we have so that we might avoid that. I'm sure you don't want a loss on your record."

"What makes you think I'd lose?" Biderhoff asked irritably.

Westberg shrugged. "If you didn't, it would be an injustice. You wouldn't want that on your record, either, I'm sure."

That gave the young prosecutor a diplomatic way out. "I'll talk this over with Jim Phillips," he said grudgingly.

"Jim is a good man," Parker said. "I think he will concur when he sees the evidence."

Parker told Westberg he would send him a bill and walked back to his car. Five yards away from the BMW, he could hear the cellular phone ringing and he hurried to unlock the door.

"Just thought you'd like to know," Morgino said, "that we found out who Aiken is."

"Who?"

"A slimeball, that's who. And a lucky one at that." He began his recitation: "Donald Everson Aiken AKA Donald Adams AKA Everson Atkins. Arrested 1979 for passing bad checks; 1981, forgery; 1983, again for forgery. He got his sole conviction on that one, pulled a year at Tehachapi. After that, he graduated to the heavier stuff. Arrests in '84 and '86 for ADW, felony assault, and extortion, charges dropped for lack of evidence. In '87, he was arrested for insurance fraud in connection with a phony car accident scam. Charges were dropped in the 'interest of justice.' Ain't that a laugher?"

"What's his connection to Barnes?"

"I don't know yet."

"Have you talked to anybody at Havenhurst? Maybe somebody there knew the guy."

"No, but I will." There was a pause. "I meant it about staying out of it . . ."

Parker had stopped listening. His attention was riveted on the white Dodge Lancer parked across the street near the end of the block. The driver was a menacing shadow behind the wheel. As if picking up Parker's thoughts that he had been made, the driver hit the ignition and the Dodge's engine roared to life. The car made a slow U-turn and turned at the next corner.

". . . Are you listening to me?" Morgino's voice intruded.

Parker's eyes remained on the corner. "Did this Aiken work with anybody?"

"There were three others in the accident ring arrested with him. Why?"

"Because I think I'm being followed." He told Morgino about the Dodge.

"Did you get a license number?"

"No."

"Next time, try to get a license number."

"Then you think I'm being followed?"

"No. I think that next time, you should get a license number."

"Thanks."

"Look, it isn't likely that any of Aiken's pals are out to whack you. Why should they? You said he was alone at Barnes's house."

"Revenge?" Parker theorized. "I *did* kill the guy."

"And he will be sorely missed by nobody. Believe me,

Doc, scumbags like Aiken don't have that kind of friends." He hesitated and something else crept into his voice, something that sounded a bit like apprehension. "But just in case, be careful. And next time—"

"I know. Get a license number."

Parker's stomach felt queasy as he hung up. If he ever got close enough to see that number, it might be too close. He hung up the phone and it immediately rang again, jangling his already jangled nerves. Steenbargen's was a welcome voice.

"I made some calls this morning," the investigator said. "Our friend Barnaby is not revered in the legal community. He's an ambulance chaser. Has a singularly sordid reputation stemming from a number of shady operations."

"Such as?"

"Well, for one thing, he was investigated for phony personal injury claims. Had a client who walked in front of buses for a living. And another with the same back problem by three different accidents."

"Ever convicted?"

"Naw. Just Law Society reprimand."

Parker's mind was working. Both Barnaby and Aiken had been involved in accident scams. Perhaps they might have bumped into each other in a mutually frequented gutter. There could be a connection, and if there was, it could be a major break. "I'm thinking of taking a run down to Havenhurst. What's on your agenda?"

"I'm at the County Clerk's Office right now, following up a couple of angles. When are you going to be down?"

"I'll meet you at Havenhurst in an hour," Parker said. "Batman to Robin, over and out."

Twenty-four

NO ONE WAS ON duty on the front desk when Parker and Steenbargen strode through the doors of Havenhurst. Beckoned by the sounds of raucous laughter and tangled conversations, they went down the hall to the dayroom, where they found forty patients milling around in a swirl of brightly colored streamers and popping flashbulbs. HAPPY 100TH BIRTHDAY PARTY, a makeshift banner proclaimed, half of it dangling off the wall.

Parker could make out two women in nurse's uniforms among the crowd, but there was no sign of Jameson.

"You want to check his office?" Steenbargen asked.

"First, let's see what the nurses have to say."

They eased into the melee and gradually worked their way toward the buffet table, on which was a giant punch bowl full of a reddish-purple liquid and hot dogs cut into tiny bite-size morsels. There was also potato salad, an assortment of puddings, and different colored gelatins with pieces of banana and orange suspended in them. At one hundred, even hot dogs were hard on the teeth, Parker supposed, if one had any teeth left to be hard on. "What did you dig up at the County Clerk's Office? Anything interesting?"

"Yeah, as a matter of fact," Steenbargen said nonchalantly. Too nonchalantly. When he acted this laid-back, the man inevitably had something truly significant to disclose. Parker knew it. And Steenbargen knew he knew it, which invariably led to the ritual of the slow leak. "I ran Katsilometes' credit report this morning. The good doctor is on very shaky ground, it seems."

"And?"

"It made me even more curious about his malpractice suits, so I went over to the clerk of the court to pull the cases."

This routine used to infuriate Parker, one of whose main virtues was not patience, but after working for years with his partner, he realized there was nothing he could do about it. The more he got worked up, the slower the leak would become. He asked casually: "And?"

"Barnaby is the attorney of record."

Parker thought that one over. "That's not so unusual. If he's the attorney for Havenhurst, that would be a natural connection."

"Uh-huh," Steenbargen said, popping a mini-dog into his mouth. "Not bad. I'm starved. Haven't had a bite since breakfast." He picked up a plate and stocked it with half a dozen more of the little morsels. Parker waited. "While I was over there, I looked up Freeze Time, just to see if they'd had any civil suits filed against them."

"Had they?"

"Three. The first one was back in 1984. A family

named Jenkins sued to recover the body of their father. They weren't suing to get the money back, just the body. They decided that the way things were going, in two hundred years the world was going to be in serious shit, and they didn't want the old man to wake up in the middle of it. Gabriel's attorney argued that the contract had been made between Freeze Time and the older Jenkins, and that it couldn't be invalidated on the whim of his offspring. He won."

"So?"

"The attorney was Barnaby."

That grabbed Parker's attention. "You're telling me that a corporate officer and major stockholder in Havenhurst is also the attorney for Freeze Time?"

"In that one case," Steenbargen said through a mouthful of hot dog. "In the other two cases since then, he wasn't the attorney of record."

"Still, it's a connection," Parker said excitedly.

"Maybe. I'd sure like to take a look at Freeze Time's incorporation papers, but they're filed in Texas. If Barnaby appears anywhere in them, or owns a significant amount of Time Freeze stock, it could constitute a major conflict of interest."

"One that might explain the inordinate number of Havenhurst patients opting for cryonic suspension," Parker said.

Steenbargen picked up a cup and ladled some punch into it. "Want me to follow up on that angle?"

Before Parker could reply, an overly rouged octogenarian sidled up to Steenbargen and asked: "You're new here, aren't you?" Her flowery perfume was so overpowering that

Parker's eyes were stinging. She had on a yellow cone hat and a cotton, flower-print dress with too many buttons undone.

"Just visiting," Steenbargen answered.

The woman's hearing aid must have been turned off, because she said: "I'm Mabel. What's your name?"

"Uh, Mike," Steenbargen answered, looking to Parker for help. But he was having trouble himself, engaged by a withered old man with vacant eyes, who had taken his sleeve and was asking his opinion of Richard Nixon. "Think he's got a shot?" the old man wanted to know.

"Well, Mark," Mabel said with a coquettish wink, "I'm in 121. Drop by sometime."

"Sure," Steenbargen said, pulling himself away. Twice more they were stopped by admiring female residents wanting to know about Steenbargen's status, and Parker, a bit astounded, said: "I never realized you had such a compelling attraction for the ladies. To what do you attribute your success?"

"The mustache."

Parker looked at him.

"It tickles."

"Oh."

A nurse at the end of the buffet table wore a name tag that identified her as "Garner." Parker introduced himself, then proceeded to describe Donald Aiken. She shook her head and said: "Doesn't sound familiar."

"He may have known Selma Barnes—"

"I knew Selma. What a shame. She was a real sweetheart. But I never saw her with anybody like that, not in the ten months I've worked here. Maybe Sally knows. She's been here for two years and she knew Selma better than I. Sally!"

The other nurse, a heavyset woman with dark hair, heard the summons and came over. Parker repeated Aiken's name and description with the same result, when a frail white-haired woman hobbled by, holding a Canon Sure Shot. "Say cheese," she ordered.

Parker said cheese, the wavering camera flashed.

"Haven't you run out of film yet?" Sally asked the old woman solicitously.

The woman shook her head. "My son just brought me five rolls. He's a good boy. He knows how much everybody here loves my pictures."

"You take a lot of pictures?"

"Oh, yes. It's my hobby."

"Ethel is Havenhurst's official photographer," Sally said, smiling indulgently. "She takes pictures of *everybody.*"

Steenbargen asked the woman: "How long have you been here?"

The woman thought, shook her head. "I don't remember exactly. Years."

"Do you keep your pictures?"

"Certainly."

"Ethel's room is known around here as 'Rogue's Gallery,' " Sally commented.

Parker caught on to Steenbargen's drift. "May we see them?"

"Of course," Ethel said, delighted.

Parker and Steenbargen followed her down the hall to her room. She liked to take pictures, all right. There must have been a thousand of them, mostly out-of-focus, tacked onto the bulletin boards that covered the walls. Havenhurst's resident population in party hats, eating, drinking, playing checkers, posing with the hired help.

Wordlessly, Parker scanned the color snapshots. Halfway down the second board, he found what he was looking for. "May I take this down?" he asked Ethel.

"Yes," Ethel said, overjoyed that her life's work was appreciated.

Parker unpinned the snapshot and examined it more closely. It was blurred, but not enough for Parker not to recognize the pock-marked giant with the mop in his hands.

He showed it to Steenbargen. "That's him."

Steenbargen looked at the photograph. "Mean-looking sonofabitch."

"Yeah." Parker turned to Ethel and asked gently: "May I keep this one?"

"For a dollar," the old lady said, unblinking.

"Wouldn't that make you a professional?" Parker asked, amused.

The woman shrugged. "Things are tough on the inside."

Parker gave her a dollar and they took the picture out to Sally. "You recognize this man?"

She gave the picture a hard look and her brow furrowed. "I'm not sure, but I think so. I think he worked here for a short time as a maintenance man."

"When?" Steenbargen asked.

"Quite a while ago. Over a year."

"Thanks," Parker said.

Parker pocketed the photograph and proceeded to

Jameson's office with Steenbargen in tow. The receptionist was absent and the door to the administrator's inner sanctum was slightly ajar. Parker tapped on it lightly, then entered without waiting for an invitation.

Jameson looked up, startled. "What are you doing here?"

"We were in the neighborhood and had a few more questions," Parker told him. "I hope you don't mind."

Jameson frowned. He obviously felt their visit was an intrusion. "What kind of questions? I thought we had disposed of the Wechsler matter."

"This is about Selma Barnes."

Jameson pursed his lips. "It was a great shock to hear of Selma's untimely demise. She was a nice woman and a fine nurse. Have they established a cause of death yet?"

"Not officially," Parker said. "But it strongly looks as if she was murdered."

Jameson made a quick movement that seemed to jeopardize his toupee's uneasy hold. "Murdered?"

"With an overdose of magnesium sulfate. Administered by a man named Donald Everson Aiken. Ever heard of him?"

Jameson ran the name through his mind. "No."

"You might have known him by another name. Donald Adams? Everson Atkins?"

Jameson shook his head. "Those names are not familiar to me." He said almost indignantly: "Why do you say I should know him?"

"Because he used to work here," Steenbargen said.

"That's absurd—"

Parker withdrew the picture and put it on the desk. "Maybe this will help."

There was a flicker of recognition. Jameson studied the picture for a long moment, then said slowly: "I know this man. But his name wasn't Aikens. It was Allison. David Allison."

"How long did he work here?"

"Briefly. A few months, perhaps."

"When?"

"Over a year ago."

"You remember the name of a man who worked here over a year ago for a couple of months?" Steenbargen asked casually.

"I remember because I had to fire him."

"What for?"

"He worked the night shift, cleaning up. Right around that time, drugs began to disappear from the dispensary. Selma reported to me that Allison was the culprit, and I dismissed him."

"Selma Barnes reported him?"

Jameson nodded. "In fact, they had a big row about it. Allison made some threats. He said he would get her for turning him in."

Steenbargen glanced at Parker. "He took a hell of a long time to get even."

Parker asked: "Did the man have any medical knowledge?"

"Not to my knowledge. Why?"

"Magnesium sulfate is an odd choice of a drug to overdose someone," Parker said. "A good choice—maybe too good—but not one a layman would normally use. Even a drug addict."

"If the man had any medical background, I certainly didn't know about it." Jameson's eyes narrowed furtively.

"How do the police know Aikens, or whatever his name is, was the guilty party? Have they caught him?"

"No," Parker said. "He'll never be caught. He's dead. He was killed last night after he broke into my house and tried to murder me the same way."

Jameson looked bewildered. "Why would he try to murder you?"

"Because I could put him at Selma Barnes's house," Parker said. "I went over there because she called me up and told me that June Wechsler might have been alive when she was taken out of here. She said Katsilometes lied on the death certificate, that he wasn't even on the premises when Gabriel and Bruce Wechsler removed her. She also said she told you about it and you told her to keep quiet."

"That's absurd!" Jameson sputtered.

"It's not true?"

Jameson's eyes darted away. "Of course not."

"Don't say anything else," a voice behind Parker said.

He turned and looked into the fisheyes of William Barnaby. "Ah. The Havenhurst attorney. And closet vice president and stockholder."

Barnaby gave him a dead look. "My association with Havenhurst is no secret."

"You didn't tell us about it."

"You didn't ask."

"I'm asking now," Parker said. "What's your connection with Freeze Time?"

"I have no connection with Freeze Time."

"Freeze Time seems to have some connection to this place," Parker said. "Three patients from here have been stored there in the last year—"

"Goodbye, gentlemen," Barnaby said, stepping away from the door.

Parker retrieved the snapshot from the desk and held it up in front of Barnaby. The lawyer's knobby eyes never moved off Parker's face. "You sure you don't want to take a look?" Parker asked. "I thought maybe you ran into him sometime back when you two were in the accident business together."

Barnaby's exterior remained unruffled. "Careful, Doctor. Comments like that make nice fodder for a slander suit. Now if you two don't vacate the premises immediately, I'll have you thrown out."

Parker and Steenbargen went. The party was in full-swing and as they angled through the room, they were stopped by Ethel, who obviously did not recognize them. She held up the camera in her palsied hands and demanded: "Say cheese."

Through clenched teeth, Parker said: "Cheeeeese."

Twenty-five

THEY TOOK ONE CAR over to the coroner's office. Ray Thompson wasn't there, but Claire Wisniewski was. She was at her desk in the investigator's room, putting on new lipstick. She finished the job before she acknowledged their presence, but Parker didn't mind. He watched in a kind of fascination. He found it very sensual.

"Back so soon?" she asked, snapping her mirrored compact shut. She slipped it into an expensive-looking eelskin cosmetics bag along with the ruby-red lipstick. Accoutrements for the fashionable coroner's investigator.

"I was in the area," Parker told her. "I thought you might have something." He indicted Steenbargen. "This is my partner, Mike Steenbargen."

Wisniewski looked at him, giving her full high-gloss lips a last gentle lick. "Hi."

"My pleasure," Steenbargen said, and sounded as if he meant it.

"You were right about the needle track," she said, getting down to business. "Merriman found it in the left femoral vein, up in the groin area. The pubic hair covered it, which is why he missed it the first time."

Parker felt a small rush of vindication. "Has he cut out the tissue around the puncture?"

"Uh-huh. Everything has been sent over to the tox lab."

"No results yet?"

"The blood and vitreous humor showed an abnormally elevated magnesium, but it'll take at least a month to get all the tissue tests run. You know the routine. Ray won't make a final determination until then."

She looked at Parker closely. "This guy must have had some knowledge of anatomy. It isn't easy to hit a femoral vein that cleanly. What was his background?"

"He was into wrecking cars," Parker said.

She shook her head and opened her mouth to say something, but was interrupted by a male deputy who rushed into the office with a distressed look on his face. "The Canadian authorities are going to send us the pilot's records, but they need to know how. Fed Ex, it'll be here tomorrow. Regular mail, it won't get here until Monday."

"Tell them to Fed Ex it," Wisniewski said without hesitation.

"Who's going to pay for it?" the man wanted to know.

"You."

"That's twelve bucks."

"You'll be reimbursed."

"How?" the young man asked, holding out his hands.

She shook her head and sighed. "Submit a chit."

The man nodded dumbly and walked away, looking unconvinced.

"Just get a receipt!" Wisniewski called after him. Then to Parker: "New guy. Hopeless." She stood and straightened her blouse and Parker was reminded of the joke about the balloon smuggler. "How do I look?"

"Fine," Parker told her, an understatement. "Where are you headed?"

"Plane crash," she said. "A guy was flying down from Vancouver in his Cessna twin, taking the family to Disneyland. Something went wrong, he clipped a radio tower, and went down in a parking lot. We have pieces of people for a block."

"Don't let me keep you," Parker said.

"Don't be shy," she said cheerfully and headed out.

Steenbargen watched her go with lecherous eyes. "I wish I'd had something like that working under me."

Parker laughed. "You'd be doing all the work."

Back in the car, the two partners reviewed the afternoon's events, trying to decide on the next course of action. "I could contact someone in Texas, have Freeze Time's incorporation papers pulled," Steenbargen suggested.

Parker shook his head. "That's out of our area. If Leah wants to dig into Freeze Time's corporate structure, she could have the investigator she has working on her mother's finances do it. Probably more thoroughly and definitely a lot cheaper."

"You suggesting we should drop it?"

Parker shrugged. After everything that had happened, he was feeling a letdown. "We've done what we were hired for. And we do have a hell of a lot of work backed up . . ."

"You're not forgetting that you were almost killed?

And that somebody might be following you around in a little white car?"

" 'Might be' being the key words," Parker said. "I'm beginning to think that Morgino is right, that I just imagined it." He argued with himself aloud: "Look, we could chase a trail of paper around until doomsday and we might be no closer to proving any collusion between Gabriel and Jameson and Barnaby than when we started. Besides, Selma Barnes's murder is a police matter now, as I've been warned, and the cops wouldn't appreciate us sticking our noses in."

"That's never stopped us before."

Parker shrugged.

"It sounds like you're making excuses *not* to press on."

"You know better than that," Parker said reprovingly.

"So what are you going to do, just sit back and wait for someone else to make a move on you?"

"No. I'm going to sit back and be damned watchful."

Steenbargen said sourly: "I guess you're right. It might be time to drop out." He got out of the car and closed the door.

"You might as well check out of the hotel," Parker told him. "See you in the office tomorrow?"

Steenbargen nodded and walked across the lot to his own car.

On the freeway, Parker phoned Leah Wechsler at her office. She sounded excited. That did little to offset the depression he felt. "I'm glad you called," she said. "Something important has come up I would like to discuss with you."

"There have been some developments I'd like to discuss with you, too."

"Good. Can we meet somewhere later? Say, around five?"

"Wherever you'd like."

"There's a restaurant on Pacific, in Santa Monica, called Shelby's. I'll meet you in the bar."

Parker said he would be there and hung up. "With bells on," he said to nobody.

Twenty-six

SHELBY'S WAS A DECO-and-rattan restaurant with French doors looking out onto the palm tree–lined cliffs of Santa Monica. Leah Wechsler was sitting at a table in the lounge, beside a fake banana plant, nursing a glass of white wine. Her hair was pulled back and she wore a white linen suit.

Parker sat down and ordered a Lite beer from the waiter. Leah asked: "So what did you want to talk to me about?"

He told her about the attempt on his life and her mouth dropped open in shock. "My God. How horrible. Could it be connected to my mother's case?"

"The police don't think so. They think Aiken killed her out of revenge for getting him fired. They're assuming he came after me because I was the only one who could possibly identify him."

She raised her glass and peered at him over the rim, her eyes questioning. "What do *you* think?"

"I'm not sure. I still don't like the timing of Selma

Barnes's murder. She was spooked about something, and it wasn't Aiken."

"You think Aiken killed her on orders from someone?" she asked, leaning forward.

"I don't know. Do you know of an attorney named William Barnaby?"

She mulled over the name, then shook her head. "No, why?"

"He is an officer and major stockholder in the corporation that owns Havenhurst, as well as being Katsilometes' attorney. A few years ago, he also acted as attorney for Freeze Time."

Her face showed excitement. "Do you realize what it would mean if we could demonstrate a business link between Havenhurst and Freeze Time?"

"At the least, a conflict of interest. At the most . . . I don't even want to think about it."

Her expression grew in intensity and she opened her purse. "Look at this."

She took out two xeroxed sheets and unfolded them in front of Parker. On each was an identical, shaky-handed signature. June Wechsler. "My investigator managed to get one of these from the signature card at the bank where mother had her CDs. The other came from a photostated copy of the contract she allegedly signed with Freeze Time."

"And?" Parker prompted. The woman, he thought, remained as much a puzzle as ever, her real identity hidden by her trauma. He was certain she would become someone else once this was over.

She paused. "I took the contract to a signature expert, along with a sample of mother's writing. He verified that it was definitely her handwriting. Yesterday, I took the copy of the signature I got from the bank to him; he verified that it, too, was her signature."

Parker put both signatures side by side. "They look the same."

"They are," she said significantly. "Too much the same. They're identical, in fact."

Parker picked up her meaning immediately. "There should be some variance—"

"Exactly! Most signatures vary in some regard, but these are exactly the same. It is the expert's opinion that the signature on the Freeze Time contract was lifted from the other document. I thought my brother was going to have a fit when I told him."

"You talked to him about it?"

"Of course. I called him this afternoon. He said I was crazy. I said it was very simple to prove that. Just produce the original of the contract. If it was signed in ink, I was willing to withdraw the accusation. He started screaming that he didn't have to produce anything and went through his usual litany of pet names he has for me. I told him I would see him in court."

Her eyes moved away. "This thing could be one giant rip-off operation. Freeze Time needs business, so it opens a convalescent home to ensure the supply. Pick patients who are senile or ones with greedy heirs, falsify a few signatures—"

"Hold on," Parker said. "Nobody has demonstrated for sure there is a link between the two businesses."

"No," she admitted. "But there *could* be. And that's what I hope to demonstrate."

"Sifting through corporate records is out of our line."

"What are you trying to tell me?" she asked pointedly.

"We're medical detectives," Parker told her. "Your private investigator could probably handle that job better than we could. And cheaper. We've done about all we can do."

She considered for a long moment. "Yes, I suppose so."

Parker reached into his jacket and removed an envelope. "Here is the affidavit. I hope it proves useful. If you need anything more, let me know."

She put it into her purse unopened. "What about your bill?"

"I'll mail it to you."

She nodded silently. Parker felt as if he were being dismissed. "Well . . ."

She said with resolve: "I'm going to nail that sonofabitch."

"Who?" Parker asked.

"Gabriel. When I think about what he did to mother . . ." Her voice trailed off and her eyes grew misty.

Parker finished his beer and left money for the check. "I guess that does it."

She shook her head and smiled faintly. "Thank you for everything you've done. It is appreciated."

"Let me know what you turn up," Parker said, rising. "I'd really like to be kept informed."

"I will."

He felt suddenly awkward and realized he was reluctant to leave her company. "If there is any other way I can be of service, let me know."

He left, wondering about the motive behind his request to be kept informed. His interest in the case was real enough—when someone tries to kill you, it tends to do that to you—but was there something else behind it, too? Was it a convenient way of keeping in touch with the woman? He was halfway to the car when it struck him. He really didn't want it to be over.

Twenty-seven

NORMALLY, PARKER THOUGHT OF his home, if not as a garrison, at least as an aid station. He went there to nurse the wounds of the day's battles, to rest, to recuperate. Tonight was different, though. Aiken's attack had violated the place. It was somehow different. Not the same haven.

He put the car in the garage, and as he went up the walkway to the house he spotted something. He bent down and picked it up. An advertising flier for "Best Way Cleaners, 20% off" had been left on the walk and someone had stepped on it only a short time before. The edge of a wet black footprint showed.

He felt it. The footprint was damp, but not the rest of the flier. He looked out at the street. Dry. Whoever had stepped on the paper had apparently crossed the lawn, which was always wet this time of day, watered by automatic sprinklers. The image of the white Lancer and the shadow at the wheel flashed vividly in his mind.

He stepped out to the street and looked up and down

the block. No sign of the Lancer, but that didn't ease his concern.

He shook his head. This was crazy. He was imagining killers everywhere. Still. . . .

He crossed purposefully to the bird-bath fountain where he kept an extra key in the water under a stone. He rolled up his sleeve, plunged his hand into the water, and confirmed it was still there.

Still not satisfied, he circled the house, checking windows for any sign of forced entry. There was none. He returned to the front and unlocked the door, leaving it ajar in case he had to make a fast exit.

The house was in the half-light of dusk. He moved through it slowly, stopping every few steps, listening for alien sounds. Still nothing. Next, he would be checking under the beds. He could not make up his mind if he was an idiot or a coward.

He went into the kitchen to make himself a drink and immediately noticed the tumbler beside the sink. He picked it up, checking to see if it was clean. At the bottom, barely visible, was a sliver of what used to be an ice cube.

Parker stood very still, listening to the house. You wouldn't think an intruder would break into a home and make himself a drink, but Parker knew different. Contrary to popular belief, criminals usually weren't too bright. The Bevins case immediately came to mind, in which the burglar had been caught and identified by the bite marks on a piece of cheese he had munched on while in the house of one of his victims.

He mentally kicked himself. He had a serious situation here and he was thinking about past cases. He pulled open a kitchen drawer and selected the biggest and sharpest carving knife he could find. He left the kitchen and started through the house slowly. Funny, he thought, he was not even really scared. Just goddamn mad.

There was nobody in the living room or guest bedroom. He tiptoed up to the closed door of his bedroom and opened it forcefully.

"Hello, Dr. Parker," Lesley Franklin said softly.

Parker let out the breath he's been holding. "You . . ."

"You were expecting someone else?" she asked, smiling brightly. His student was stretched out on the bed, wearing her horn-rimmed glasses and nothing else.

"Yes," Parker said, finally managing to speak. "You don't happen to own a white Lancer . . . ?"

"You spotted me, huh?"

"I spotted you," Parker said, relieved. "Where is it now?"

"Around the block. I thought you might have noticed it—and I *did* want to make this a surprise."

"Don't worry, it was a surprise," Parker said, taking time to examine her body. It looked even better than it did in jeans and a figure-hugging blouse, and certainly better than in a surgical smock.

"How did you get in here?" Parker asked.

"The key in the birdbath. That's a super hiding place. Took me all afternoon to find it."

"You opened the door and put it back?"

"Yes."

"Careful girl."

"A girl can't be too careful."

Parker paused. He was annoyed, yet at the same time

flattered. He had never met anyone quite so brazen, but he was enjoying the view. "So what's supposed to happen now?"

"I was hoping we could get to know each other better. You could, for example, get out of those clothes."

For a moment, Parker was tempted. It would be a very pleasant way to unload a day's burden.

Lesley ran her hand down her sleek shape. "Come on, Doctor. It's good for you."

"That much I know."

"Then what are you waiting for?" she asked softly.

Good question, Parker thought.

She stretched, arching her back, raising her breasts. Her legs opened in the same movement. "I find you very, very sexy," Lesley said, holding his gaze.

"This will do nothing for your grade," Parker told her from the doorway.

She laughed. "I didn't think it would."

"Then why?"

"Let's just say I have a thing for older men."

Great. Maybe he shouldn't have asked. He stood staring, undecided. Until a woman's voice said behind him: "Hello?"

Parker swung around to face Mia, who had just stepped into the bedroom, and now, her face ashen, was looking past him, to the bed.

"How long have you been here?" Parker asked stupidly.

"I just arrived," Mia said, her eyes flashing fire. "And I guess I won't be staying." She started to leave, then turned back. "How long has this little tryst been going on?"

"It isn't. This isn't what it seems."

"It never is," Mia said, always one for the exit line.

Parker followed her outside, and finally caught up with her at her car. "Will you listen to me?"

"No," she said, fuming. "Just . . . leave me alone."

"I can explain," he said, grabbing her arm.

She turned and faced him with an icy stare. "I'll bet you can."

"That girl broke into my house—"

She smiled tautly and nodded. "Right."

"It's true, goddamn it—"

Mia shook her head sadly. "I'm beginning to think Eve is right about you."

That stopped him. "Eve? What's she got to do with this?"

"Eve is the reason I came over. She and I had a nice talk today. I was surprised to find that she wasn't quite the bitch you always depicted her. Actually, I found her quite nice."

"What did she say about me?"

Mia's eyebrows jumped. "Don't flatter yourself, Eric. You weren't the main topic of discussion, believe it or not. Ricky was."

Parker frowned. "What about Ricky?"

"She agreed to let you have Ricky per your court agreement, no more screwing around. And maybe more often if it works out."

"Why?" Parker asked suspiciously. "What's the catch?"

"No catch. I convinced her that she might be doing the boy more harm than good by letting her feelings toward you spill over into your relationship with him. She realizes that it could be psychologically harmful for him to be denied a father figure, someone who can help guide him." She looked beyond him, toward the house. "Now, I'm not so sure. I don't know if he's old enough to grasp that his father is a baby raper."

That dampened Parker's momentary joy at hearing about his son. "That girl is a medical student in my forensic pathology class."

Mia stuck out her lip. "Don't tell me. She brought you an apple."

Parker sighed in exasperation. "I don't know what her problem is, but she has been following me around. She let herself in with the key in the birdbath. When I got home, I found her like that."

"A coed crush," she said, her voice dripping sarcasm. "Isn't that cute?"

"It's the truth," Parker persisted.

The anger seemed to dissipate from her features, and she said in a coldly distant tone: "It doesn't matter, Eric. This is just a symptom of what has been going on between us for some time."

"What is that supposed to mean?"

"We've been going through the motions, but we've been kidding ourselves. There isn't much left for us."

Parker shook his head, but he knew that she was right. "Look, Mia—"

She cut him off. "We're too alike. Maybe that's our problem. We're both too wrapped up in ourselves and our work to give enough to someone else."

Hearing the harsh truth, Parker felt strangely sad. He remained silent, knowing that offering arguments, denials, would not change things. He had failed miserably at every relationship he had ever had, except his work. This was just one more.

He released his grip on her arm and she got into her car.

"Thanks for talking to Eve," Parker said.

"I didn't do it for you," she said. "I did it for Ricky." She paused and looked up at him. "Don't blow it, Eric."

She fired up the Porsche and Parker said: "I'll call you."

Mia just shook her head, gunned the engine, and took off down the street.

Lesley was nowhere in sight when Parker entered the house. He made himself a stiff drink in the kitchen, then went into the living room and turned on the television, but not the sound. Charles Bronson was shooting some muggers in one of the later Death Wishes.

Lesley came out of the bedroom, dressed in tight jeans and a white pullover sweater. "I'm sorry if I messed things up for you."

"It was probably already messed up."

"I didn't know you had a girlfriend. You look like a loner. Maybe that's what made you so interesting."

Parker didn't say anything.

"Mia Stockton. Wow."

Parker rubbed his forehead. "Would you mind getting out of here?"

"You're sure you want me to?" she asked, smiling crookedly.

Actually, Parker was not sure at all. But he said: "Yes."

She started to go, then turned back and asked sheepishly: "What you said about this not affecting my grade—does that still go?"

She withered under the coldness of Parker's stare and scurried out the door.

Parker had intended to pore over the Ennis material again, searching for a solution to the dilemma he faced, but the double-surprise visit had banished any inclination he had for work. Women. You can't live with them and you can't shoot them.

He took a slug from his drink, turned up the volume on the television, and sank into his easy chair to watch Bronson kill a few more people. He was in the mood for a little mindless violence.

Twenty-eight

PARKER MUST HAVE DOZED off, because he was awakened by the phone. He picked it up, looking at his watch at the same time. Nine-twenty.

"Dr. Parker? This is Leah." Her voice sounded strange, tentative.

"Hi."

"I just wanted to let you know, that I, uh, I've decided to drop the entire matter of my mother's death. I'm discontinuing the investigation, so there is no need for you to do anything more about the matter."

Parker was confused. He'd told her he was off the case and now she was calling him to tell him he was off the case? He was about to say something, then stopped. Something was very wrong here. "May I ask you what led to this decision?"

She said haltingly: "I was . . . wrong about everything. I had a long talk with my brother. He showed me the original of the contract mother signed with Freeze Time. I have no doubts now that she wanted the suspension process.

I've decided that it's not for me to try to thwart her last wishes."

"You talked to your brother?"

"Yes. We decided this petty squabbling is only destructive to both of us. He has agreed to split up the inheritance."

"Kind of a change of heart for him, isn't it?"

"I suppose it is," she said. "But he saw that otherwise, whatever mother did leave would only be eaten up in court costs."

"Where are you now?" Parker asked.

"Home."

"Is he there, too?"

"No."

"Are you sure you wouldn't like to talk this over?"

There was a long pause.

"Leah?"

"Yes, I'm quite sure. I've mailed you a check for an additional $5,000. I imagine that should more than cover any additional expenses you incurred above your retainer."

"That's very generous, but I don't think the total will come to that much. I can have my secretary prepare an itemized bill tomorrow—"

"No," she said abruptly. "I'm leaving in the morning on an extended vacation. To Hawaii."

"Hawaii? This is kind of sudden, isn't it?"

"Things have been piling up," she said. "With all that has happened in the past few weeks, I feel like I need a break. I just want to lie around a beach for a while and relax and try to forget about everything."

"How long will you be gone?"

"I . . . I don't know."

Parker waited.

"Well . . . goodbye. And thanks for everything."

Parker was listening to a dial tone. He put the phone down slowly and stared at it for a good ten seconds before picking it up again. She picked it up on the second ring. "Hello?"

"Leah, this is Eric Parker."

"Yes?"

"Are you all right?"

Her voice grew taut. "Yes. Why do you ask that?"

"You sound a little strange."

"I'm fine."

He paused. "What airline are you flying out on?"

There was a muffled sound. "Delta."

"What time?"

"Nine A.M."

"I can see you off—"

"Don't bother," she said weakly.

"It's no bother," he insisted. "By the way, I believe we have an incorrect home address for you in our files. Can you give that to me now?"

There was another pause. "3670 Eames, Encino 91305."

He wrote it down. "Got it. I'll bring that affidavit to LAX tomorrow morning, just in case you want it."

"Fine," she said stiffly.

"Goodnight, then."

"Goodbye."

Parker replaced the receiver again, threw on a jacket, and went to the car. His troubled thoughts would not leave him alone on the thirty-minute freeway ride over to Encino.

Eames Drive curved its way beneath a canopy of thick

elm trees, into the hills overlooking Ventura Boulevard. Number 3670 was representative of the other homes on the street, a modest split-level ranch-style house, the kind that was popular in the late 1950s around Southern California. Lights were on in most of the houses on the block, but not in Leah's. The house was dark and there were no cars in the driveway.

Parker pulled over to the curb on the opposite side of the street and turned off his ignition. Grabbing the flashlight from the seat next to him, he got out of the car and went around to the trunk. From the spare tire compartment, he selected a short metal jack handle, testing the weight of it in his hand. It could easily break a bone if it connected in the right spot, he decided. He would have much rather had a gun, but since he didn't own one, this would have to do.

As he walked across the street to the house, he kept his eyes on the darkened windows, wondering if he was being watched from behind them. The windows themselves seemed to be skull-like eyes, black and empty. He went up the brick walkway to the front door and rang the bell. If anything had happened, he would have been surprised. That was not how déjà vu worked.

Crickets sang from the bushes, happy to be alive, however briefly, on this lovely evening. Down the hill, traffic on Ventura Boulevard made hissing sounds, like the surf lapping the shore. A motorcycle buzzed up the hill, then turned off. He listened to its motor fade, then rang the bell again.

Parker took a deep breath and went to the side gate beside the garage. He reached a hand over and pulled the cord that lifted the latch and opened the gate. The outside door that opened into the garage was ajar and Parker pushed it open with his foot and stepped back, the jack handle hoisted in readiness. After standing there like that for what seemed a long time, Parker began to feel stupid, and inched cautiously toward the door.

The only thing in the garage was a white Chrysler LeBaron convertible. He tried the passenger door and when he found it locked, shone his flash through the window. There was a small box of tissues on the front seat, nothing much else in the front or back.

The door on the other side of the garage opened onto a glassed-in back porch and terrace that looked out onto the small backyard. The porch was crowded with patio furniture and planters of white magnolias that filled the air with their sweet, syrupy scent. The smell of the blossoms was so thick it was almost overwhelming, like the cloying, suffocating perfume of old ladies.

Parker went to the sliding glass door that led into the house. Curtains were drawn across it, obscuring any view inside. He tried the door, but it was locked. He paused and looked around, trying to decide what to do. After ten seconds or so of deliberating on it, he shrugged and swung the jack handle.

The breaking glass sounded like a major explosion and Parker wheeled around, sure that the entire neighborhood had been alerted that there was a housebreaker at work on the block, and that the phones at the local police station were ringing off the hook. He stood frozen, waiting for shouts of alarm, dogs barking, the sound of distant sirens, but there was nothing.

He stuck the flashlight into his back pocket and reached tentatively through the hole in the glass, the jack handle poised in his sweaty palm, just in case someone grabbed his hand from the other side and tried to pull it through. His fingers found the lock and snapped it back, and he retrieved his hand gratefully, then pulled back the door.

His stomach fluttered nervously as he pushed his way blindly through the curtains, which stuck to his face like a spiderweb. Nobody hit him, no hands grabbed him, as he freed himself from the fabric and snicked on his flash. His beam swept the living room, located a standing lamp, and he went over and turned it on.

The living room was of medium size, furnished sparely in low-slung modern. The floor was wood, covered occasionally by an island of throw rug. A large flagstone fireplace occupied one wall, and across from it was a three-stooled bar done in blond wood. At the end of the bar, a small, deco-looking pendulum clock ticked loudly as it made its arced swing.

"Leah?!"

The ticking of the clock was the only sound in the house. To Parker, it sounded like a bomb, ready to go off. He turned on lights as he moved through the house on tiptoe, his weapon poised, ready to strike at any shadow that moved.

He peeked quickly into the small dining room and adjoining den and went into the kitchen. Everything there seemed in its proper place. He went back out through the living room and down the short hallway that led back to the bedrooms. Two small bedrooms there shared an adjoining bath. Neither of them looked as if it had been occupied in some time. Parker felt a twinge of trepidation as he reached for the light switch on the wall of the third and last room and flicked it up.

Light flooded the room, spotlighting a queen-sized bed covered with a black satin spread flanked by two blond wood nightstands, a blond wood bureau, and a rattan chair. Parker moved quickly around the end of the bed and looked between the bed and the wall and felt a wave of relief to find nothing there. He let out the breath he was holding and relaxed the grip on the jack handle. He was alone in the house.

He stood, surveying the room. At the foot of the bed, the spread was rumpled carelessly, as if someone had sat or placed something heavy there. On one of the nightstands lay a paperback copy of a Dean Koontz novel, a bookmark protruding from its midsection. Parker thought about that, then opened the drawers of the nightstands. A prescription bottle of Xanax. Another of Midol. Dental floss. Kleenex. A small flashlight.

He went to the closet and opened the door. There was a large gap in the clothes hanging there. Two Tourista suitcases stood on the shelf above. There was also a gap between them, wide enough for another suitcase the same width. Parker's eyes dropped to the floor. A large selection of shoes were placed neatly, side by side. There were no gaps there.

The clothes in two of the bureau drawers were dishevelled, as if someone had pulled items out of there in a hurry. He went into the bathroom. A toothbrush stood in a glass by the sink, next to an array of beauty products, makeup and makeup removers. The shelves of the medicine cabinet held toothpaste, a razor, a bottle of Tylenol, a can of Edge shaving gel. In the drawers was an assortment of hairbrushes and combs, bottles of nail polish and polish remover, hairpins, the usual female stuff.

Parker turned off the lights and went back down the hall to the den. The floor-to-ceiling bookshelves were crammed with hardcover and paperback novels, as well as nonfiction on various subjects. On top of the mahogany desk, looking rather conspicuous between the desk calendar and the telephone answering machine, were a Delta schedule of flights and a color travel brochure of Hawaii. He stared at the brochure for a moment, then hit the playback button on the answering machine. He listened to the silent tape for ten or fifteen seconds before shutting it off.

The desk drawers contained the usual stuff office desks contained—stationery, pencils, pens, paperclips, stamps, envelopes. The two-drawer filing cabinet beside the desk held neatly labeled hanging files—Payables, Banking, Insurance. He glanced through each, but there was no sign of the papers she had shown him in the restaurant. Her attaché case seemed to be gone, also. Perhaps she had taken it to her office. Maybe that's where she was now, finishing up some last-minute work. No, that made no sense. How did she get there? Her car was in the garage.

Parker glanced down at the phone. It was a Computaphone, one of those with a memory that stored the last number that had been dialed. Parker picked up the receiver and punched the "Redial" button and the telephone automatically began to dial. From the amount of numbers, it was obvious that the call had been long distance.

On the fourth ring, a man answered: "Freeze Time."

Parker said nothing.

"Hello?" the voice said.

Parker replaced the receiver gently. He went back through the house, turned out all the lights, and went out the way he had entered.

Twenty-nine

IF ANYONE WAS COUNTING, the girl had said forty-six words in a row that would never, under any circumstances, appear in *Vogue,* although given a new couturier, she might appear there herself. She was a beauty, Parker thought, but maroon velvet hotpants and black knee-length boots were definitely not *in* this year, except on Sunset Boulevard, which was, coincidentally, where she had been picked up. The L.A.P.D. plainclothes vice detective who had brought her in did not seem in the least bothered by her string of descriptive epithets. He went on impassively typing out his arrest sheet, occasionally pausing for a sip of coffee from a Styrofoam cup.

Across the desk from Parker, Morgino hung up the phone and rocked back in his chair. On the squadroom wall behind the detective, a sign said in large block letters: YOUR LUCK HAS CHANGED TODAY.

"Well?" Parker asked.

"Leah Wechsler boarded Delta flight 1040 at ten tonight, bound for Honolulu."

Parker turned back to face him. "She told me she was leaving tomorrow at nine."

Morgino shrugged. "Her reservation was originally for that flight, but she changed it."

"Rather suddenly. Kind of odd, don't you think?"

Morgino picked up his coffee mug and leaned back in his chair. "I think most things women do are odd."

As if echoing Morgino's thoughts about the battle of the sexes, the girl in the hotpants loudly challenged the plainclothes vice detective booking her for prostitution to engage in some biological acts with himself that were impossible for an earthman. The girl looked no more than fifteen and probably wasn't. They grew up fast in Tinseltown. They died fast, too. Parker had seen plenty of that. Much too much.

He turned his attention back to Morgino. "I told her I was going to see her off, that's why they changed it."

"And who is 'they'?"

"Gabriel and his people. She was forced to make that call. They took her."

Morgino shrugged. "A free trip to Hawaii, she can't bitch too much."

"They didn't take her to Hawaii."

Morgino's eyebrows jumped. "No? Where did they take her, then?"

"Freeze Time," Parker said.

"How do you figure that?"

Parker leaned forward. "Leah Wechsler has a computerized phone with a memory. I pressed the redial button and it rang Freeze Time. That means the last call made on her phone was to that number. Now, you tell me why she would call me, *then* call Freeze Time, at that time of night?"

Morgino slurped his coffee. "I can't. Why don't *you* tell *me*?"

Parker said excitedly: "It wasn't her calling, that's why. Somebody from Freeze Time was calling headquarters to let Gabriel know everything was okay and they were on their way."

Morgino blinked. "Who was on their way? What in the hell are you talking about?"

"They took her," Parker said, waving his hands in exasperation. "Look, Leah was getting too close to nailing her brother and Gabriel for fraud. She had proof that her mother's signature on her contract with Freeze Time had been faked. She argued with her brother about it earlier in the day. They knew she would keep on until she exposed them and they knew they had to stop her before she did. They forced her to call me up and say she was dropping the whole investigation, then they took her."

Morgino tossed up a hand. "You're forgetting one thing. One person can't be two places at the same time. Leah Wechsler got on a plane for Hawaii."

"You don't have to show identification to buy a ticket and get on a plane. They wanted to make it look like she was going away, so that nobody would miss her for a while—"

Morgino said dubiously: "So they packed a bag for her?"

"They had to make it look real, in case I or somebody else checked. Only they screwed up. They took clothes, but forgot to take any shoes. What woman do you know is going to take a dozen outfits to Hawaii and one pair of shoes?"

Morgino shook his head incredulously. "Look, Doc, I know you've been through a lot lately. That Aiken thing has you spooked, and I can see why—"

"Aiken had worked for Havenhurst," Parker interrupted. "And Havenhurst and Freeze Time are connected."

"You have no proof of that."

"It's the only thing that makes sense," Parker insisted. "That's why Selma Barnes was killed, not because of any personal grudge. She was going to spill the beans and somebody found out about it."

Morgino sighed, his eyes drifting over to the booking area where the night's dregs were being processed. It was shaping up to a big night for vice, a constant parade of hypes, hookers, and pushers as the cops busted their asses to remove them from the streets for a day or two. He turned back to Parker. "I'll tell you what makes sense. The woman was telling you the truth. She and her brother had a reconciliation and she decided to celebrate her newly acquired inheritance by taking a nice vacation."

Parker shook his head vehemently. "She hated his guts."

"Money can smooth over a lot of hate."

"Are you going to get a search warrant for Freeze Time?"

Morgino made a face. "On what evidence?"

Parker made a choppy, frustrated gesture with his right hand. "What I've told you!"

Morgino grimaced. "I'm supposed to roust a judge out of bed at midnight and tell him that I want him to sign a search warrant on the basis of information given to me by a man who has admitted breaking and entering a woman's home? Despite the fact that there is no sign of violence on the premises, no evidence that there has been a kidnapping? A woman who, according to the airline computer, is in Hawaii? Because she forgot to take her shoes? He'd ream me a new asshole."

"You have to do *something,*" Parker insisted.

"Maybe, but you don't," Morgino said, still angered by Parker's foray into Havenhurst against his specific orders. "I know it doesn't mean much to you, but I reiterate, and I hope this time it sticks—this is police business. We'll take care of it."

Parker was adamant. "How?"

The detective took on the look of a desperate man searching for desperate solutions. "If you'd get the hell out of here, I'd have time to think about that."

"Check the hotels in Hawaii," Parker urged. "I'll bet you don't find a Leah Wechsler registered in any of them."

"We can do that. And we can question the stewardesses on the flight, see if one of them remembers the woman—"

"That'll take days. By then, it'll be too late."

Morgino shrugged. "I can't do any better than that, unless you come up with something more solid, Doc. Sorry."

From his car phone, Parker called Steenbargen's home.

"What's up?" the investigator asked sleepily.

"A lot. Get dressed and I'll fill you in when I get there."

"Where are you now?"

Parker looked out the windshield at the lighted skyscrapers of downtown L.A. "Hollywood Freeway heading south. I'll be at your place in fifteen."

"I'll be waiting."

Thirty

KATSILOMETES' HOME WAS A small gray-white knob clinging to the shrub-covered hillside like a cancerous growth. It had to be one of the first summer houses built in Laguna. The lot was the only value now, but that would be very substantial. On a clear day, the view would stretch to Catalina and beyond.

"You're sure this is the place?" Parker asked, staring in disbelief. It looked like something transported from an East L.A. slum. Rickety wooden steps climbed to a sagging porch lit by the faint-green sickroom glow of a low-watt bug light. Beyond, shutters sagged. "Six-four-six?"

Steenbargen dug into his pocket for the slip of paper on which he'd scribbled the address. "Six-four-six." He half-turned to glance down the hill. Coming up in the dark, with no street lights, it had been like a maze. "Providing we're still on Lookout."

"Who knows?" Parker said, although he was reasonably certain.

Steenbargen pointed to the white 450 Mercedes parked in the dirt driveway. "That's his car."

Parker read the license plate. "KATSY. Cute."

"The dollies must think so. At least until they get up here."

"Yeah," Parker said, looking again at the dilapidated house. "I guess you weren't kidding when you said the guy had some money problems."

They got out of the car and went up the steep stairs to the dark house. Steenbargen rapped loudly on the torn screen door and when nothing happened, rapped again. A light went on in the house and a minute later, the front door opened a crack. A sleepy eye peered out at them. "You . . . What the hell do you want?"

"We need to talk to you," Parker said.

Katsilometes yanked open the door. He had on a blue terrycloth robe and his hair was mussed. He said angrily: "What the hell time is it, for chrissakes?"

Parker checked his watch. "One-ten."

"You have your goddamn nerve—"

"It's an emergency."

"What emergency?"

"Let's talk inside," Parker said, pushing his way inside. Steenbargen followed.

"Hey!" Katsilometes protested. "Get the hell out of my house!"

The two men ignored him and continued into the small living room. The place was a mess. Papers, dirty glasses, and empty pizza boxes littered the tables. The old and worn furniture looked as if it had been procured at half a dozen different garage sales. Nothing matched.

We are down to the truth, Parker thought. No more front. No slick office, no fancy car, no gold chains. Just the plain unvarnished fact of a man in trouble. Katsilometes' anger turned to embarrassment as Parker and Steenbargen took in the place, and he said in a softer tone: "What do you want?"

"You could be in serious trouble," Parker said.

Katsilometes' eyes narrowed. "Trouble? What are you talking about?"

"The Wechsler case."

Katsilometes' tanned face blanched. His mouth opened, then closed. "What about the Wechsler case?"

Parker sat down on the lumpy couch and leaned back. "How interested are you in staying out of jail?"

Katsilometes stared silently.

"I'm trying to do you a favor, Doctor. When all the pieces come together, everybody is going to go down for murder, unless someone is smart enough to make a deal."

"Murder?" Katsilometes said tautly, fighting to retain his composure. "This is ridiculous—"

"Is it?" Parker asked.

Katsilometes' knees grew weak and he sunk slowly into an easy chair. "June Wechsler died of natural causes . . ."

"I wasn't talking about June Wechsler. I was talking about Selma Barnes. She was murdered by a man named Donald Aiken, who used to work for Havenhurst. She was killed because she was going to give me the details of the connection between Havenhurst and Freeze Time."

"I don't know what you're talking about," Katsilometes said, rubbing his nose.

Parker glanced at Steenbargen, who was smiling.

"I think you do. Havenhurst solved a basic problem for Gabriel. Volume. There are only a few hundred cryonics adherents in the country. To make it truly pay, he needed to increase his support base. Havenhurst did that nicely. Old people who have no living relatives, or whose relatives would gladly part with $100,000 or so, just to speed up the dying process."

Katsilometes shook his head and said weakly: "That's not true . . ."

"You signed all the death certificates, Doctor. You're in it up to your neck."

Katsilometes' tan seemed to have permanently faded as the blood had drained from his face.

"June Wechsler was alive when she was taken out of Havenhurst," Parker said.

"No."

"I have incontrovertible proof," Parker bluffed.

Katsilometes' eyes widened. "What kind of proof?"

"I'll let the cops tell you when they pick you up in the morning."

"You're lying! You have no proof."

"Your only chance to save yourself is to turn state's evidence," Parker said. "Where did June Wechsler die? Freeze Time?"

"I'm telling you, she died at Havenhurst. I have witnesses—"

"Selma Barnes was a witness," Parker said. "She's dead."

"I had nothing to do with that."

"Maybe not directly, but Aiken was under orders from somebody. That could tie you into a conspiracy charge."

Katsilometes ran a hand through his hair and whined: "Why are you persecuting me?"

"I'm not persecuting you," Parker said. "I'm trying to

help you. Because if you don't come clean now, you're going to be an accessory to another murder."

Katsilometes' head snapped up. "What are you talking about?"

"Gabriel has Leah Wechsler."

"The daughter?"

Parker nodded. "She came up with some very damning evidence. Proof that her mother's signature on her contract with Freeze Time was forged. She made the mistake of telling her brother, who must have told Gabriel. Gabriel realized he had to get rid of her before she turned over what she had to the police, so he took her."

"Where?"

"The logical place is Freeze Time. They can do what they want to her there."

"He wouldn't kill her," Katsilometes said weakly.

"It's the only way he can be sure of silencing her," Parker said. "Murders have a funny way of multiplying. One leads to another."

Katsilometes' eyes had the look of a trapped animal.

"Where did June Wechsler die?"

The man seemed to deflate in front of them. "Freeze Time."

"You were there?"

"Yes."

"There's only one reason you would be at that time of night. You cut off her head."

"The woman was brain-dead," Katsilometes said desperately, as if trying to convince himself.

Steenbargen shot Parker a knowing glance. "Why did you do it? For the money?"

Katsilometes glanced. "Why else? Look at me. I'm a drowning man."

"Not quite yet, but you will be if you don't help us now. If Leah is killed, I'll make damned sure you are prosecuted as an accessory to murder."

Katsilometes shook his head. "The way this all started, it was nothing," he complained quietly. "It was just a way to make a few extra bucks. Nobody was supposed to get hurt. Just a few extra bucks."

"Save your own ass," Parker advised. "Because the others are going down."

Katsilometes sighed heavily. "What do you want me to do?"

Thirty-one

THE STATION WAGON ROLLED to a stop in front of the dark building and Katsilometes killed the engine. The two Rottweilers immediately ran to the Cyclone fence, barking furiously.

Katsilometes hesitated, then got out of the car and went to the gate as the dogs repeatedly hit the fence. He pressed the buzzer and after a while, a man asked: "What is it?"

"Dr. Katsilometes. Is Gabriel here?"

"He left about an hour ago. He's due back anytime now."

"I have an emergency patient here from Havenhurst," Katsilometes said. "Storch. She needs immediate attention."

"Nobody called us."

"There wasn't time. I happened to be there when she deanimated."

"I have to beep Mr. Gabriel—"

"Fine, but do it after you give me a hand with the body," Katsilometes shouted over the dogs' barking. "I have to get her inside and on a perfusion unit immediately!"

The halogen lamps mounted on the roof of the building turned on, flooding the yard with their bright light, and Reid came through the door. His hair was tousled from sleep and he was barefoot, dressed in a blue T-shirt, jeans. He shouted the heel command and the two dogs came to immediate attention. He chained them up on the other side of the yard, then came over to the gate, yawning.

"Why the fuck do they always have to croak in the middle of the fucking night?" the big man said grouchily as he unlocked the gate.

Katsilometes didn't answer, but opened the back of the wagon. They lifted out the covered gurney and set it on the ground, and Katsilometes rolled it through the gate to the front door. "Anybody else here?" Katsilometes asked when they had gotten inside.

Reid hesitated. "No," he said finally, then looked at Katsilometes closely. "Something the matter with you, Doc?"

"No," Katsilometes said quickly. "Why do you ask?"

"You're sweating. You look kind of sick."

Katsilometes turned away, trying to hide his nervousness. "I'm fine."

Reid reached a hand toward the zipper on the plastic body bag. "Storch, huh? Let's take a look."

In a jerky motion, Katsilometes grabbed the man's wrist. "I've packed her in ice. Open that and it'll be all over the floor."

Reid withdrew his hand, obviously not wanting any extra cleaning chores at this time of the morning. Katsilometes said: "Let's get her into the OR."

Reid nodded and opened the door to the laboratory corridor. They rolled the gurney inside, past the gleaming rows of stainless-steel dewars, into the operating room. Katsilometes said: "Go call Gabriel. I'll prep her for perfusion."

Katsilometes waited until Reid had gone out, then unzipped the body bag. Parker's head popped out and he gulped in a lungful of cool air. He unzipped the bag the rest of the way and wriggled out of it like a moth shedding a chrysalis. "Damn, it's hot in there," he complained, plucking at his perspiration-soaked shirt.

"He'll be back soon," Katsilometes said nervously. "Hurry up."

Parker hopped off the gurney, thrust his hand back into the body bag, and pulled out a short crowbar. The place was eerily silent, except for the sounds of pumps and the soft steady hum of refrigeration.

He pushed open the door that led into the kennel room. Several of the dogs began to bark and Parker's attempts to shush them were totally ineffectual. A quick look around told Parker Leah was not in there.

"Where would they keep her?" Parker whispered.

"I don't know."

"I just hope we're not too late."

They went back out through the OR and stopped at the door. Parker peeked around the corner. Reid was coming across the lab with a large-bore automatic in his huge fist.

Parker frantically waved Katsilometes back through the OR into the kennel room and began unlatching the cage doors of the half-crazed animals. Dogs and cats noisily bolted for their freedom and Parker and Katsilometes ran out of the other door, into the empty corridor, to the back stairs.

Behind them, Parker could hear Reid swearing as the

animals streaked around him, barking and yowling. Parker took the stairs by twos, half-listening for the sound of Reid's footsteps behind them, to the door of Gabriel's office. The door was locked. Parker jammed the crowbar into the door frame by the lock and pried it open. The lock gave way with a bang and the door swung open, and Parker stepped inside and turned on the light.

Except for the furniture, the office was empty.

"She's not here," Katsilometes whispered. "You were wrong!"

Parker shook his head. "She's here somewhere. We've missed her."

He led the way out of the door, down the front stairway. He hit the door at the bottom and they were in the main corridor once more. Parker stopped on the other side of the closing door and listened. Reid's heavy footsteps were right behind them, pounding down the stairs. He quickly glanced down the long corridor, gauging the distance. The man was too close; they would never make it to the lab. It was now or never. He flattened himself out alongside the door and poised the crowbar.

The door slammed open and Parker concentrated, bringing the bar down as hard as he could on the man's right forearm. The gun clattered to the floor as Reid screamed in pain and clutched the shattered bones above his wrist.

Parker stooped and snatched up the Browning 9mm, while the big man continued to moan. "You broke my fucking arm!"

"Sorry about that," Parker said, not very sincerely.

Katsilometes, who had chosen not to make a last stand,

and was halfway down the corridor, now turned and hurried back.

"I need a doctor, goddamn it!" Reid cried.

"You have two of them right here," Parker said. "But first, we want Leah Wechsler. Where is she."

"Fuck you," Reid spat. "I don't know what you're talking about—"

"I'm talking about the gas chamber, Reid. I'm talking about felony fraud, murder, conspiracy, and kidnapping. Gabriel is a dead man. The whole operation is collapsing in on him. Katsilometes has already told me what he knows. Pretty soon, everybody will be pointing fingers. By then, the D.A. won't care about making any deals, Reid. You'll fall with Gabriel. Don't be a fool, save yourself."

Reid's face contorted as he struggled with his options.

"The cops are on the way," Parker urged. "It's all over. Make your choice now. When they hit that door, it'll be too late."

Reid made up his mind. "Okay. "

He led them past the lab, where a black mongrel dog barked at a hissing cat, which was precariously perched on top of one of the dewars, to a steel door at the end of the corridor. Parker held the gun on Reid while Katsilometes lifted up his T-shirt and removed the set of keys from his belt. Katsilometes flipped through the keys and Reid stopped him when he got to the right one. He unlocked the door and pulled it open.

The room was a twenty-by-twenty concrete-walled storeroom that held half a dozen four-foot-tall stainless-steel tanks marked LIQUID NITROGEN. On the cement floor next to the tanks, Leah Wechsler lay unconscious. Katsilometes bent down and felt for a pulse, then tried shaking her gently. She moaned quietly and tried to roll away. Katsilometes looked up at Parker. "She's been drugged."

Parker asked Reid. "What was she given?"

"Pentobarbs."

"How much?"

"Just enough to put her to sleep until Mr. Gabriel decided what he was going to do with her. She'll be okay."

Parker said to Katsilometes: "Go get the gurney. We'll take her out on it."

Katsilometes nodded and turned to go out, then stopped suddenly and backed into the room. Gabriel stepped through the doorway, holding a Mac-10 machine pistol. Tagging behind him was Bruce Wechsler. Gabriel leveled the nasty-looking machine gun at Parker's midsection and said: "Going somewhere, Dr. Parker?"

Parker froze. "Little heavy on the artillery, aren't you, Gabriel? Don't tell me that's for animal rights activists?"

"And for other nosy intruders," Gabriel said. "Reid, get his gun."

Reid snatched the Browning from Parker's grip with his left hand. "The bastard broke my arm," Reid complained. His face was very pale and covered with sweat. He was going into shock.

"You'd better get him some medical attention," Parker suggested.

"In good time," Gabriel said.

Katsilometes' eyes were wide with fear. "He made me bring him here, Gabriel. He knows all about Havenhurst and about June Wechsler being alive—"

Gabriel silenced him with an icy glance, then turned his attention back to Parker. "You disappoint me, Doctor.

You really do. I expected you to have more vision than the rest of the medical community. I thought you would be able to appreciate what we are trying to accomplish here."

"Like murder and fraud?"

Gabriel shrugged. "Sometimes drastic sacrifices are needed to achieve great dreams."

"Human sacrifices? Like Selma Barnes?"

"The woman should not have meddled in our business."

"So you had your boy Aiken shut her up," Parker said. "The magnesium sulfate your idea? It wasn't bad. It might even have been perfect, except he made the mistake of trying it twice."

"That was not our doing," Gabriel said calmly. "The man acted on his own. Unfortunately, Aiken couldn't get it out of his head that you could identify him."

"I'll bet he was a valuable employee while he was alive," Parker went on. "Not only was he willing to eliminate human problems for you, his talents for forgery must have made him a handy man to have around when you had to duplicate signatures. Where did pick him up, from one of Barnaby's accident rings?"

"You're very bright."

"Is that your silent partner? Barnaby? Is that who helped you set all this up?"

Gabriel smiled mockingly. "Barnaby? Don't be ridiculous."

"He's a major stockholder in Havenhurst—"

"Barnaby is a merely a nominee. He signed over his stock over a year ago."

"To whom?"

Gabriel didn't answer.

"Somebody had to fund all this," Parker said. "You

didn't get the money for all this equipment from doing high colonics."

Gabriel's expression turned deadly serious. "I don't know if I like the sarcasm in your voice."

"Really?" Parker said tauntingly. "Well, tough shit, Superman."

Gabriel looked amused. "I don't think you realize, Doctor, what a spot you are in here."

"You're the one in a spot, Gabriel," Parker said. "You're finished. My partner is outside in a car and right about now he should be dialing your number on the cellular phone. If he doesn't like what he hears, he will immediately call the police. Ask Katsilometes."

Gabriel looked questioningly at Katsilometes, who nodded. "He's telling the truth."

"Reid," Gabriel said. "Go check the closed-circuit monitors. See if you can spot a car outside. And turn the dogs loose. It might buy us a little time, just in case he is telling the truth."

Reid nodded weakly and went out.

"He's driving around. You won't be able to see him."

Gabriel smiled at the apparent ruse.

"Look, I'm out of this, Gabriel," Katsilometes said firmly. "I can't be a party to murder—"

Gabriel grinned. "You already are, you fool."

"Me?" Katsilometes sputtered.

"June Wechsler. You cut her head off, remember?"

White was showing all around the irises of Katsilometes' eyes now. "You said she was brain-dead!"

Gabriel shrugged. "So I lied."

Parker took a step back. He was stopped by something solid and cold. A tank of liquid nitrogen.

"But I didn't *know,*" Katsilometes groaned.

"I'm afraid ignorance is no excuse for murder," Gabriel said. "So you can see, you're in this with all of us."

Parker said to Bruce Wechsler, who had remained passively in the background, "What do you think of that, Bruce? This man, your revered guru, murdered your mother."

Wechsler shrugged and said, as if by rote: "It was a mercy freezing."

Parker stared at him in disbelief.

"She was dying anyway. There are numerous advantages in freezing someone before the disease can run its final course. By picking the time and place of suspension, we can reduce the patient's suffering, as well as enhance the possibility of revival."

"You can't be serious," Parker said.

"Oh, but I am," Wechsler replied in a cool, confident voice Parker had never heard before. "My mother and now my sister will be making cryonics history. Leah will be the first perfectly healthy human being ever to be cryonically suspended. It could increase drastically her chance of being revived at a future date. Who knows? She might wake up in the year 2200 and thank me for it."

Reid came back into the room and said: "No sign of any car." He was unsteady on his feet. The gun in his hand wavered and he looked as if he was going to be ill.

"Do it somewhere else," Wechsler snapped at him.

Gabriel looked uncertainly at his prize follower, and said: "What do you think about this partner business, Bruce?"

Wechsler started at Parker for a moment. "He's bluffing."

"I don't know," Gabriel said. "Why would he come here without—"

"Shut up," Wechsler told him.

It was only then that the realization hit Parker. "It's you. You're the one behind it all."

Wechsler's fat lips formed into a grin. "Why are you so amazed? Because of what Leah told you about me? She never did give me any credit."

Parker turned dumbfounded to Katsilometes. "Did you know about this?"

Katsilometes shook his head, bewildered.

Wechsler suddenly looked immensely pleased with himself. He puffed up like a blowfish. "Leah is a lot like my mother, as much as she would like to deny it. She always thought that I was weak and stupid, too. Mother wanted to think that, to keep me at home, by her side, the sick, dependent bitch. That was fine with me. I cultivated the image, used it. Then, behind the scenes, I started making my own plans."

"Those bad investments she made, they were your idea," Parker said.

"That's right. I set up a series of dummy companies and talked her into investing her money. Then, I siphoned off the money to C.E.D., Inc., my own land development corporation, and started up Havenhurst."

"That way, you'd rake in the money while the patients were alive and after they died."

"Correct."

"Where did you find Barnaby?"

"Money has a tendency to bring all types of people together," Wechsler pontificated. "Attorneys like Bill have a particularly keen nose for it."

"He helped you set up the dummy companies?"

"That's right. Although his specialty was personal injury law, he had enough of a background in corporate law and legal chicanery to be an immense help."

"So you installed him and Jameson as the front men at Havenhurst, then found Gabriel to dummy for you as the mastermind of Freeze Time, while you remained the devoted follower and mother's boy."

"Perfect, don't you think?" Wechsler said, grinning with his own self-importance.

"Almost. Except for Leah."

The grin turned into a frown. "Yes. My dear sister. She had to stick her goddamn nose in. Hired that meddling little private investigator to start rummaging through mother's financial records, then hired you to get that goddamned autopsy done. She was a constant thorn in my side. She would have kept digging until she uncovered the whole thing. She had to be eliminated."

Parker picked up the bitter emphasis in the man's words. "Why were you so opposed to an autopsy? What were you afraid we'd find?"

"When the toxicology results are in, I believe they'll show significant amounts of lead in my mother's tissues."

"The Alzheimer's," Parker said, fighting the urge to look at his watch. Steenbargen should have called by now.

Wechsler said nothing, but smiled sardonically.

"You fed her lead over a period of time, knowing it would simulate the symptoms of Alzheimer's, and once you got that diagnosis, you could put her in Havenhurst and get rid of her once and for all."

"The bitch would have lived until she was ninety," Wechsler explained calmly. "I couldn't wait that long."

"How do you propose to explain away the toxicology results?"

Wechsler shrugged. "I don't. When notified, I will be shocked, like everyone else. An examination of the tap water at the house will show a dangerously high contamination of lead from the pipes."

"And how come you haven't been poisoned as well?"

"I, as everyone knows, am a health-food nut. I only drink purified, distilled water."

"You can't think the police are going to let it go by," Parker said.

"I wouldn't have had to think about it at all," Wechsler said resentfully. "But you had to butt in. You've brought all this on yourself, Doctor."

Parker felt the cold metal at his back. He glanced back at the valve on the tank, just above his left shoulder. It was covered with frost. He was getting nervous. Wechsler was obviously not the most stable of personalities. He could order his dummy Gabriel to open fire at any time. What in the hell was Steenbargen doing? He tried to keep the man talking. "You don't really believe in any of this stuff, do you? You're just in it for the money?"

Wechsler laughed. "What else is there?" He looked at his watch and said: "It looks like your partner forgot to call. It doesn't matter, anyway. By the time the police get a search warrant, you and my sister won't be here."

Parker didn't like the sound of that. "Really? Where will we be?"

"I'll put Leah on ice for a while, excuse the pun," he smirked. "You . . . I think an automobile accident might be in order."

"Arranged by Mr. Barnaby—"

"The man does have his uses."

Katsilometes shook his head and said in an emotional tone, "I can't be a party to this. This is cold-blooded murder."

Wechsler eyed Katsilometes with obvious disdain. "Don't be a fool. This man is a threat to your life, as well as ours. He can send you to prison for the rest of your life."

"You don't think this man is going to let you witness a couple of murders and walk, do you, Katsilometes?" Parker said. "I'll bet he has plans for a passenger in this car accident he's planning—"

"That's enough talk, Parker," Wechsler said sharply. Then to Gabriel: "Take them out to the car."

Gabriel waved the barrel of the Mac-10 to the door. "Let's go."

Parker gauged Gabriel's distance. Eight or nine feet. Reid stood behind him, a little off to the right. He shook his head. "I'm not going anywhere. You might as well give it up, because you can't get away with it—"

"I'm telling you to move! Now!" Gabriel growled.

Somewhere in the building, a phone rang. Gabriel reacted instantly, his head snapping around, and Parker knew it was now or never. With his right hand, he reached over his left shoulder and turned the valve on the tank behind him, dropping to the floor in the same movement.

Gabriel caught the motion out of the corner of his eye and pivoted, swinging the Mac-10 around just as the high-pressure blast of liquid nitrogen gas shot out of the nozzle like a rocket exhaust. A deafening spray of gunfire filled the room and Parker lay flat on the floor and covered his head with his hands as bullets ricocheted off the floor and walls.

Suddenly, the blasting ceased and there was only the whooshing sound of the freezing gas. Slowly, Parker looked up. He could see nothing but the white plume, shooting twenty feet into the hallway.

He crawled over to the tank and felt his way up the metal cylinder, careful to keep under the spray, and shut off the valve. Everything was deadly quiet. Parker inspected himself for bullet holes, miraculously found none, then walked through the dissipating freezing white mist to where Gabriel still stood, looking very much like a snowman with a gaping mouth. He had opened his mouth to scream, but nothing had come out, his vocal cords freezing instantly as the deadly-cold blast hit him in the face. His eyelids had frozen open, too, which meant that if he lived, he would undoubtedly be permanently blind.

Parker tried to take the gun, but his hands recoiled from the icy metal. It would have been no use to him, anyway. Once Gabriel had pulled the trigger the first time, his finger had been frozen in position, and the automatic had continued to fire until the clip had emptied.

Parker looked around for Katsilometes and spotted him lying in a heap in the corner. He had been hit by at least half a dozen slugs, four of them in vital places. He was dead. Parker scrambled over to Leah Wechsler and found that she, like him, had escaped injury. He felt for a pulse and determined her vital signs were still strong. Then he remembered the other men in the building.

He got up and went cautiously to the door and peered into the corridor. Reid was seated on the floor opposite the door, his back propped up against the cement wall, unconscious. Gabriel had shielded him from the direct force of the blast, but the right side of his face and his right arm were badly burned from the liquid nitrogen. Parker glanced up and down the hallway, but there was no sign of Bruce Wechsler.

The automatic was lying a few feet away, and Parker went over and picked it up. It was cold, but not freezing. He shivered. The temperature in the place had dropped sixty degrees in a matter of seconds.

The phone was still ringing and Parker ran into the lab and picked it up. "Yeah."

"Jesus Christ, you took long enough," Steenbargen said worriedly.

"I could say the same thing about you," Parker grumbled. "That was the longest twenty minutes in history."

"You okay?"

"Yeah. Call the cops. Tell them to bring an ambulance. We have some dead and injured here."

"Who's dead?" Steenbargen asked urgently. "Leah?"

"No, she's okay. Katsilometes got it, though. Gabriel's dead and Reid is in pretty bad shape. Where are you?"

"Around the corner."

"Keep an eye out for Bruce Wechsler. He got away. He's the mastermind behind this whole crazy setup—"

"Wechsler?" Steenbargen asked in surprise.

"Yeah. And listen, Mike, don't try to apprehend the sonofabitch. He's desperate and he may be arm—" Parker stopped as he glanced up at the TV screen that monitored the outside yard. Wechsler lay very still on the ground by the front gate. He was on his back, his groin and half his face gone. Standing over him very proudly, the two Rottweilers, Damien and Shaitan, waited for their reward for a job well done. "Never mind," Parker said.

Thirty-two

"THE DEFENSE CALLS DR. Eric Parker," Sheldon Roth said.

Jim Gordon scowled disapprovingly at Parker as he walked past him on his way to the stand. Parker glanced over at the handsome, immaculately groomed young man at the defense table. Ennis had been here before and he knew how to play the game. Wear a suit and tie, brush your hair, smile ingenuously, and keep that wide-eyed look of innocence on your face. No jury would ever think that a kid that looked like that could possibly be capable of inflicting such horror on another human being. Ennis smiled and winked surreptitiously, and Parker felt a wave of anger break inside himself. He would not let it show, however. On the stand, he would remain, as always, the cool, rational expert. Punks like Ennis were not the only ones who had had experience with the system and knew how to use it.

After he was sworn in, and his jury-dazzling qualifications as an expert in forensic pathology were cited—his many degrees, his experience as a pathologist for the county of Los Angeles for five years, his six years as chief coroner, his past presidency of the National Academy of Forensic Science—Roth got on with the matter at hand. "Dr. Parker, you have had an opportunity to go over the autopsy reports on Sally Beckworth, as well as had access to the prosecution's exhibits in this case, have you not?"

"Yes, I have."

"And you have heard the testimony of Dr. Fennell, who did the autopsy, as well as that of Mr. Wykoff from the Los Angeles Sheriff's crime lab, who testified about the trace evidence allegedly linking my client, Mr. Ennis, to the murder of Sally Beckworth?"

"Yes, I did."

"Now, as has been noted, Dr. Fennell originally estimated the time of death of Sally Beckworth to have been around five-thirty P.M. on the night in question, an estimate he later revised to nine, after it was found out that Mr. Ennis had been seen by several witnesses at an AM-PM Minimart around seven that night—"

"Objection, Your Honor," Jim Gordon shouted. "Mr. Roth is trying to infer that Dr. Fennell changed his testimony to fit the prosecution's case—"

"Objection sustained."

Roth smiled, bowed to the judge, then to Gordon. "I certainly did not mean to impugn Dr. Fennell's integrity. I am simply trying to determine how such a gross discrepancy in time could have been made." He turned back to Parker. "Dr. Parker, in the autopsy report, it states that partially digested remnants of a hamburger and french fries were found in Ms. Beckworth's stomach at the time of the autopsy."

"That is correct."

"How long would it usually take for food to pass out of the stomach, once it is ingested?"

"Normally, about two hours." Parker kept his eyes on the face of the killer at the table. Ennis seemed to be loosening up now. A smug smile crossed his lips, as if he were beginning to enjoy this cat-and-mouse game.

Roth turned and took two steps away, tapping the pencil he held in his hand in his palm. "It has been determined that Sally Beckworth ate a last meal of a burger and fries at approximately five o'clock, on her way home from school. It would seem to follow then that the original estimate of her death at five-thirty would seem more reasonable than that of nine o'clock, would it not?"

Parker shook his head. "Not necessarily."

Roth balked. "Pardon me?"

"Two hours is the normal time it takes food to move out of the stomach into the duodenum. That is if a person eats and lives *normally*. But any physical or emotional disturbance can upset the process drastically. If someone was being assaulted, frightened, or tortured, digestion can proceed very slowly. Even stop completely. Sally Beckworth was tortured, and most certainly was frightened. It's altogether possible that she died at nine. Or anytime after five-thirty."

Roth obviously had not been expecting that answer and he walked back to the defense table to regroup. The smile was gone from Ennis's lips now, and his eyes were narrow slits, watching Parker. Roth picked up a paper from the table. "The lab results on the semen sample taken from the vagina and panties of the victim showed that the killer was an ABO Type A secretor, with genetic markers of GLO I and PGM 2 + 2. That is consistent with Mr. Ennis.

The state's expert witness testified that it is also consistent with ten percent of the Caucasian male population. Did you have an opportunity to examine the semen sample, Dr. Parker?"

"No."

"Why not?"

"The sample from the girl's panties had been used up in the lab tests."

"What about the semen found in the girl's vagina?"

"PGM was confirmed by an independent test, but unfortunately, GLO could not be tested for accurately, due to contamination."

Roth nodded knowingly at the jury, as if he had just made a point. "The state's expert witness also testified that the partial hair found on the dead girl was 'consistent with' Mr. Ennis's hair." He whirled around. "Is it not true, Dr. Parker, that a comparison of a partial hair is practically useless? That a single, complete hair can vary drastically from its follicle to its end?"

"By normal testing procedures, that is true."

"What do you mean by 'normal testing procedures,' Dr. Parker?"

"Visual microscopic comparison of the hairs in question."

Roth smiled complacently. "And that was done in this case, was it not?"

"No, it was not."

The smile evaporated from Roth's lips. "What do you mean, 'it was not'? You heard the prosecution expert testify that was the means by which he compared the hair from Sally Beckworth against the hair taken from Mr. Ennis."

"That was the test Mr. Wykoff used," Parker said, sitting back confidently. "I used another test."

The attorney balked, trying cautiously to gauge the significance of this unexpected turn. He sensed something was amiss, but he had no choice but to go on. The jury would find it strange if he suddenly dropped the line of questioning. "What test did you use, Dr. Parker?"

"A polymerase chain reaction test."

Roth frowned. He had no idea what Parker was talking about. "And what is this test?"

"In laymen's language, it is a test that duplicates DNA codes in a test tube, just as they would be duplicated in a human body. If a sample is too small for normal testing, as was the partial hair found on the Beckworth girl, it can be run through a machine called a thermal cycler, which extracts the basic genetic code from the sample and amplifies it. Once that is done, the sample can be typed."

Parker looked over at Gordon, who watched in fascination, also trying to grasp this latest revelation.

"You're telling me," Roth said, frowning, "that you had this test run on the hair found on the Beckworth girl?"

"Yes. Dr. Weisenthal at USC Medical Center ran the test."

Roth could do nothing but ask the question. "And what did the test show?"

"That the hair found on Sally Beckworth was identical to the hair of the defendant, Lamar Harold Ennis."

There was a rustle from the jury, and Roth turned abruptly to Judge Tandy, a wizened thirty-year veteran, who ruled his court with an iron hand. "Your Honor, may I approach the bench?"

While Gordon and Roth went to the bench for their

conference, Parker took the opportunity to glare at Ennis. The smugness was gone now, replaced by bewilderment. The game had slipped from his grasp and he no longer understood the rules. From the witness box, Parker could hear Roth's barely controlled whisperings: "Your Honor, I knew nothing about these tests. The witness did them on his own."

Gordon broke in: "But Counsel, it's your witness."

Tandy said: "Mr. Gordon is quite right."

Roth protested: "Judge, you know that DNA typing is not admissible in California courts yet—"

The judge shrugged. "I'd be happy to tell the jury to disregard your witness's testimony, but you're going to have to explain why it is not to be allowed. Or get another witness to tell the jury why it is not admissible. Proceed."

Gordon went back to his table and Roth approached Parker, looking troubled. "You realize, Dr. Parker, that DNA testing is not admissible in California courts?"

"I know it has not been admissible up to this time."

"Isn't DNA testing not allowed in courtroom testimony because it is a highly new field, and therefore unreliable?"

"No, I don't believe so. It is being used in many states currently and in other countries. It's just a matter of time before it is used in California. In my opinion, it is a very accurate test."

Roth shook his head in defeat. The damage had been done and he would only amplify it if he continued. "I have no further questions for this witness."

Jim Gordon stood and said, "I would like to cross-examine, Your Honor."

Gordon stood behind the table and asked loudly: "Dr.

Parker, in your expert opinion, the hair found on the body of Ms. Beckworth came from the head of Mr. Ennis?"

"Yes."

Gordon rubbed it in, glancing at the jury to make sure they got it: "That is unequivocal?"

"Unequivocal."

"And as an expert in forensic science, have you formed an opinion as to the guilt or innocence of Mr. Ennis?"

"I have."

"Would you share that opinion with us?"

Parker glared at the young punk at the table, who was staring at him with hot, unmitigated hatred. "I think he's guilty as hell."

Gordon beamed. "Thank you, Doctor. No further questions."

Outside in the sunshine, even the grimy L.A. air seemed somehow cleansing. In spite of the fact that it might cost him some business in the future, he felt very good about what he had done. A small victory, perhaps, but in this life, you had to take them where you could get them.

A red Firebird pulled over to the curb out front of the Criminal Courts building, and he recognized it instantly as Eve's. He walked over and bent down. Ricky was sitting in the passenger seat. "Hi," Parker said.

"Hi," the boy said, rather sullenly, it struck Parker.

Eve leaned over and said: "Mike told me where you were. I was coming this way, anyway, so I thought I'd drop Ricky off with you here."

"Fine," Parker said enthusiastically. He opened the door and Ricky got out, looking as if he would rather be somewhere else.

I'll change all that, Parker thought. This was going to be the weekend that was going to turn everything around. Or at least it would be a beginning. He lifted the boy's canvas bag containing his weekend things out of the back-seat and said: "I got Laker tickets for tonight. Front row."

That seemed to cheer the boy up a little. He was an avid Laker fan.

"Then, tomorrow, we can do anything you want."

"Sounds good, Dad."

"We'll have a great time, wait and see." To Eve, he said: "I'll drop him off Sunday night. And thanks."

"Don't thank me," she said. "Thank Mia."

That would be difficult to do, Parker thought, considering the woman had not accepted the half-dozen phone calls he had placed to her during the past two weeks. Not that that made him totally unhappy. After considerable thought, he had come to the conclusion that Mia had been right, that it had been over for them a while ago. The problem would be explaining that to Ricky, who was Mia's number one fan. He hoped the boy liked Leah—whom Parker had been seeing quite a bit of lately—half as much, although he doubted he would. Lawyers were not nearly as exciting as TV stars.

The Firebird sped off and the father and son went across the street to the lot where Parker's BMW was parked. As he pulled out of the lot, the phone rang.

"I just got a call from an attorney in Miami," Steenbargen said. "He has a doctor client whose wife disappeared from the ship while they were on their honeymoon cruise. The woman's body washed up in Biscayne Bay two days later."

"So?"

"The autopsy showed she drowned, but I guess she was pretty bruised up. On the basis of that, the Dade County Coroner ruled the death a homicide, and the cops arrested the husband."

"Just on the basis of some bruises?"

"Apparently so."

There was a pause. Parker sighed. The slow leak again. "So?"

"The attorney wants another opinion."

"I don't blame him."

"In fact, he wants another autopsy, pronto."

"Let him petition the court for one."

"He wants you to do it."

"Take his name and tell him I'll call him back on Monday," Parker said.

"The body is going to be buried tomorrow."

"Out of the question," Parker said adamantly. "This is my weekend with Ricky—"

Steenbargen said casually: "The doctor, I guess, is an old friend of yours from medical school. Sidney Metz?"

The name shook Parker. He hadn't seen Sidney in years, close to ten, probably. "That's ridiculous. Sidney wouldn't kill anyone."

"That's what the attorney says," Steenbargen said.

Parker thought about it and shook his head silently. He would like to help, but it was out of the question. This weekend was going to be a new beginning between him and his son. Then he thought about what his best friend had told him while they were jogging: "You have to find a way to make Ricky part of your life."

He turned to Ricky and asked: "You liked going on the set with Mia, didn't you?"

The boy's eyes lighted up. "Gosh, *yes*. Can we go there this weekend?"

"I don't think she's shooting this weekend," Parker said, offering up a fatherly smile. "But I'll tell you what: How would you like to visit the set of *Miami Vice*?"